"I admit that it is a delicate matter, perhaps even indelicate, but in no way thoughtless, I do insist—to greet the reader with the classic journalistic line of: 'If you were going to read only one book this year, here you go, this is the one.' "—*Le Journal Littéraire*

"Those who decide to read this book on a bus or a train should be forewarned: uncontrollable bursts of laughter will seize you at any time!"—*Library Journal*

"Clever. . . . There's plenty of fun to go around, and it is a pleasure to be led by Mr. Roubaud."—Colin Walters, *Washington Times*

"Quirky, mischievous, off-the-wall . . . Roubaud is not your ordinary writer. And that's his extraordinary [...]

"Impishly fantastic." —*Atlantic Monthly*

"*Hortense Is Abducted* gives a resolutely new perspective on a reality which we wonder afterwards if all the other novels we have read have not lied about."—*Le Soir*

"Although *Hortense Is Abducted* is a mystery with a plot literally as intricate as a sestina, its real fascination lies in Jacques Roubaud's conversational asides, inside jokes and self-referential wordplay. . . . A good deal of amusement."—*New York Times Book Review*

"For Jacques Roubaud, writing is a game, thus an activity that is as serious, amusing and codified as mathematics or the physical sciences. The author chooses his reader as partner . . . and begins by telling him a charming tale. . . . The result: you are won over by a powerful, irresistible *joie de vivre*, a delight in laughter. And in reading."—*Telerama*

Books by Jacques Roubaud in English Translation:

The Great Fire of London

Hortense in Exile

Hortense Is Abducted

Our Beautiful Heroine

The Plurality of Worlds of Lewis

The Princess Hoppy

Some Thing Black

HORTENSE IS ABDUCTED

JACQUES ROUBAUD

Afterword by the Author

Translated by Dominic Di Bernardi

Dalkey Archive Press

Originally published by Éditions Ramsay, 1987
Copyright © 1987 Éditions Ramsay
Afterword copyright © 1989 Jacques Roubaud
English translation copyright © 1989 Dalkey Archive Press
First paperback edition, 2000

Library of Congress Cataloging-in-Publication Data:

Roubaud, Jacques.
        [Enlèvement d'Hortense. English]
        Hortense is abducted / Jacques Roubaud; translated by Dominic Di Bernardi. — 1st ed.
        Translation of: L'enlèvement d'Hortense.
        I. Title.
        PQ2678.O77E713   1989   843'.914—dc 19   88-30390
        ISBN: 1-56478-256-5

Partially funded by grants from the National Endowment for the Arts, a federal agency and the Illinois
Arts Council, a state agency.

Dalkey Archive Press
www.dalkeyarchive.com

NATIONAL
ENDOWMENT
FOR THE ARTS

Hortense Is Abducted

Contents

Part One

Murder at Sainte-Gudule

Chapter 1

The Thirty-Three Strokes of Midnight

The weather was warm and beautiful, so we couldn't have been in Belgium. All was quiet that evening around the Church of Sainte-Gudule. In the vegetable garden, at the foot of the Poldevian Chapel, the snails gently chewed the heads of lettuce. The Gudule Bar, opposite the church, in Rue des Grands-Edredons, had cleared out its last drunkard and put away its green plants. The petits fours were asleep in the window of the Groichant Bakery, opposite the parishioners' exit, on Rue des Citoyens. All was quiet in the Square des Grands-Edredons. The sandbox was empty. Not a light in the windows of the six staircases (A, B, C, D, E, and F) at number 53, nor on the square, nor on Rue Vieille-des-Archives. The only illumination was shed by the stars and the full spring-time moon, mocking the city streetlamps. Black were the green plants of the Gudule Bar; black the leaves of the trees in the square; white and piss yellow the sand in the sandbox; dark blue the sky at the bottom of the fruit bowl of stars. Not one car, not one T-line bus (optional stop) came to disturb the meditative silence of the streets (nor the silence of the meditating streets, for that matter). Not a soul, not a cat. Not the soul of a cat, consequently. The sounds of the city arrived only faintly, as if from far away, as if come from another world: the world of anguish, of the ephemeral, of illusion; the world that is barbarous, carnivorous, villainous; the world of fevers, beavers, bacterium; of biles, of woes, of crimes; the world of dementia, of embolism, of entropy; of lucre, of licentiousness, of smoke; of lycanthropy, of pyromania, of

3

syzygy; and reciprocally ... you know, *the world*. It was a moment of inexpressible gentleness (but which we have just, nevertheless, expressed, with a rare felicitous phrasing).

All the same, without unduly lingering on a description of this idyllic location (it is not going to remain so for long), let us place ourselves in thought on the sidewalk, at one of the two corners where meet Rue des Grands-Edredons and Rue des Milleguiettes: the right-hand corner, if you have your back to the square, as we do at this very moment.

Just who is this "we"?

By "we" I mean quite precisely:

a) *You*, my Reader: there is room for *one* reader, representing the crowd of my dear, innumerable future readers. You'll excuse me for choosing only one among you, but how would you all be able to stand together on the corner of Rue Milleguiettes? It's so narrow! In the days of my mad youth (I mean my youth as an Author, for I had already attained a respectable age), at the time of first starting out in the noble but exhausting career of a novelist, I had saddled myself with a Narrator. This was not out of any desire for originality, nor any concern for modernism, which is quite far removed, believe me, from my preoccupations. It was out of scruple, of modesty. I wished in a way to disappear behind the characters of my tale, so as not to trouble them, so that they might feel free. So that the adventures might move forward all by themselves, in *their* truth. By the way, I recount only true things: I loathe inventing, and I do not know how to lie. But lo and behold, the character of the Narrator in the book I'm speaking about, my first novel, because I had unwisely permitted him to say "I" like all narrators, got caught up in the game. He said "I," then "I myself," then "Me"! In a word, he did not leave off saying "I" and didn't let me get in a single word. Furthermore, he proved himself to be, as the novel progressed (toward its final climax full of unexpected twists and turns), tremendously insolent. Such pretension! He constantly

4

intervened to contradict me, claiming he knew better than I what was happening. He shifted the course of events to give himself the best role. And he even ended up by publishing his own version of the story, accusing me of errors, omissions, lies, plagiarism! I decided to make do without his services, to rid myself of him as Narrator. But, let me be clear on this point, *only* as Narrator. You will see him here as a Character, and he will get only what he deserves, believe me.

b) *Me.* Here's the reason there are two of us at the corner of Rue des Milleguiettes for the beginning of this terrible story, and not three (but, as the English say, two's company, three's a crowd).

Let us place ourselves in thought on this hot sidewalk. We remain motionless for a moment, invisible and silent in the great nocturnal silence under the springtime moon. Invisible, unspeaking, but seers, united. (If "I" is an Other, is it not None-Other than you, Reader, *mon semblable, mon frère!*) Let us place ourselves in thought on the sidewalk of Rue des Milleguiettes; then, from that point, let us stride ten or so yards down the narrow street, and press (mentally) upon the series of buttons composing the (secret) entrance code PL 317. Let us push the heavy ancient door. And let us enter. Let us cross the courtyard, go into the garden. Let us pause for a moment to study the small villa, the two floors occupying the rear. This is Père Sinouls's residence, organist at Sainte-Gudule, and his family's. But for the moment the family is not there. It's spring vacation: Madame Sinouls is visiting her own family; the Sinouls girls, Armance and Julie, are gallivanting around: one gallivanting blondly (Julie); the other, redheadedly (Armance). The Sinouls boy, Marc, is playing bass viol in Japan. Père Sinouls is by himself. He is snoring away.

. . .

In the silence of the nocturnal night (the qualifier "nocturnal" with which night is here embellished means that we have at hand a genuine night, deep, nighttidal, a truly nightish night), in the silence of the nocturnal night, back within the Sinouls house, someone moved. (Warning: it is *not* Père Sinouls. Père Sinouls is asleep *and* snoring, activities which, unlike Gerald Ford, he is able to conduct both at once and simultaneously.) Yet someone in the Sinouls house woke up, stretched, shook himself off, rose to his feet, pushed open the perron door, went down into the garden. Advancing through the garden nocturnally bathed in moonlight, someone sniffed the rosebushes, took a few steps, yawned, farted, yawned again. The nightingale sang in the linden tree. A patrol of six ants (led by a lieutenant ant serial number 615243 [this lieutenant was not one-legged, ants having more than two legs, but x–1-legged]) headed across the path of the sunflowers toward the raspberry bushes. Someone (the someone we are speaking about) walked round the garden. The door was open. He hesitated a moment (henceforth, and barring express mention until the end of the chapter 3, this someone will be designated by "he"), then, shrugging his shoulders (in a gesture which meant, in all likelihood, "And, after all, why not?") crossed the courtyard and, passing under the porchway, approached the entrance door. It, too, was open.

(And who had left it open, in defiance of the strictest regulations of the jointly owned property, not to mention the rules of the most elementary safety? Who, I ask you? But *you*, my dear Reader, *you*, while I preceded you under the porchway to show you the way. You, who also left ajar the door of the Sinouls garden. It is *you*, Reader, who performed such acts, with incalculable and tragic consequences, don't forget it!)

Before the heavy, large entrance door to the street, he hesitated again longer. He did not really think it would be open. He had come that far mechanically, without much confidence. The street held him, its mysteries: the smell of the street, the square, its bushes, all of it irresistibly attracted him. But at the same time, he was scared. Silly to say, he was scared of a cat. Not of any cat in general, but of one cat, of one quite particular Cat. This cat had reigned over the neighborhood during the course of another story, which preceded this one (in every story, you have certainly noticed, as I have myself, there is always another story, the one preceding the story, and that's why it's so awfully difficult to tell stories); and this story here is, consequently, the sequel of the story preceding it. This cat was named Alexandre Vladimirovitch. Alexandre Vladimirovitch, who so frightened him, had not, certainly, reappeared in the neighborhood for several months. He had disappeared on the day a street, Rue de l'Abbe-Migne, was dedicated, actually a street-segment stolen from Rue des Milleguiettes, and located opposite it like an asphalted remorse, on the other side of the Square des Grands-Edredons. He knew this, and yet he was scared. But in the end, the temptation was stronger. He went out into the street and soon found himself in the square: alone and free.

At that moment, the bell of Sainte-Gudule began to toll. Standing still, he started to count on his fingers the slow and majestic strokes of the bell that passed through the silence, the moonlight and the night. The last time they had sounded, it was eleven o'clock. And since it was eleven o'clock, he had counted eleven strokes of the bell (he was a remarkable bell-stroke counter). And now he was awaiting, with a light, happy shiver (he was not scared anymore), the twelfth stroke of midnight before continuing his clandestine stroll. There were nine strokes (and beforehand, there had been eight, and before that seven, and still before that six, but I do not mention them to avoid pointlessly overloading this paragraph), there were ten strokes, there were eleven. Next there were twelve strokes, naturally and . . . . *he froze on the spot, suddenly seized by an incommensurable terror: the thirteenth stroke of midnight tolled.*

.　.　.

I wrote: *the thirteenth stroke of midnight tolled*, and at once I ask myself: are we still dealing with midnight? If twelve strokes signal midnight, what might the cause be for thirteen? Into what world are we projected by this supernumerary stroke? Into what unknown dimension of space and time? These are rather serious questions that are not mine to resolve, but which I owe it to the Reader to raise.

He froze on the spot, seized by an incommensurable terror. And now not only was there a thirteenth stroke at midnight, in defiance of all plausibility, of all custom, but this thirteenth stroke was immediately followed by a fourteenth, by a fifteenth. And at each new stroke of the now accursed bell, his paralyzing, horrifying, far worse, horrifyingly coruscating terror redoubled. Interminably, new strokes of midnight shattered the silence, doubling his terror each time. Mechanically, he counted them. He continued to count, fascinated and incredulous, on his ten fingers: fifteen, sixteen, seventeen, eighteen, nineteen, ... The bell tolled thirty-three strokes, then stopped. Prey to an abject fear, he stood as if petrified. His terror, already striking him powerfully since the sound of the thirteenth bell, now attained an intensity 2 to the power of 20 times stronger, since it had doubled at each new stroke. If T was the intensity of the initial terror, it was now T', and T' amounted to 2,097,152 if our calculations are correct.

Let us take advantage of his terrified stillness to offer a very simple, not at all supernatural explanation of the phenomenon: for some months, due to the tourist trade, the pastor of Sainte-Gudule, with the tacit accord of his hierarchical superior, Monsignor Fustiger, had decided to have the clock of the church rung in the old style, as in the old days, by real bell ringers. And he had hired for this purpose (upon the recommendation of Père Sinouls) two celebrated Burgonian (as was said long ago) bell ringers, Molinet Jean and Crétin Guillaume, famous musicians and specialists of this peerless art, campanology. However, on precisely this night, the first of the novel, Molinet Jean and Crétin Guillaume had felt like sleeping peacefully and granting themselves seven hours of well-deserved rest. But since their professional conscience was unfailing, they had not wanted to dispense with a single of the bell strokes for which they were contractually obligated to Sainte-Gudule. Thus they had rung them, but *all at once,* following the twelfth ordinary stroke of midnight. Then they had left to go to bed. That indeed came to, if I am not mistaken, $1 + 2 + 3 + 4 + 5 + 6 + 12$ strokes, that is, 33 in all.

(On this subject, since you felt compelled, in order to find the correct number and verify that I was not deceiving you, to add to 12 the sum of the 6 first whole numbers, allow me to interject an amusing anecdote: the story goes that one day, in eastern Prussia, at the end of the eighteenth century, the precise date being determined by the tale, the teacher of the small school where young Gauss found himself . . . but I will go no further: it has been brought to my attention that we are not here in order to recount the history of mathematics, but that we are dealing with a NOVEL.)

The bell fell silent and he (I am speaking, in accordance with the conventions of the still anonymous "he" that we have been following since the beginning of the fourth paragraph, not of young Gauss) stood paralyzed with terror for a long while. When he was once again in a condition to move, his only thought was to get back as quickly as possible to the place he ought never to have left: home. But, at that exact moment, he heard a horrible noise in the bushes. And this noise issued from somewhere between the place where he found himself and Rue des Milleguiettes. The way back, the path of salvation, was cut off. Hightailing it, he then fled along Rue de l'Abbe-Migne. Still running (with us behind, but we're not what he is hearing, for we are as silent as we are invisible) he turned left, back behind the church in Rue des Citoyens.

He ran, he ran: until exhausted and out of breath, he stopped.

He looked around him: nothing was moving. A bit reassured, he began to walk again, by a path as roundabout as it was curvilinear, wanting to get back to the Sinouls house without recrossing the square.

Finally, the door of the house was in sight: quivering with relief and impatience, he rushed toward it. But suddenly, there opposite him, a shadow: someone. But this was someone he knew, it was a friend. Overjoyed he went toward him, prepared to greet him, when something made him draw back, a doubt, a premonition. Raising his eyes, he perceived the horrible hellish vision of death. A ghastly cry caught in his throat, tightening with anguish. He took off running toward the Poldevian Chapel, his last possible refuge, land of asylum.

Too late!

There was a shot, a death rattle.

The nocturnal lunar silence of the nighttidal night fell once more. Again all was quiet around Sainte-Gudule: not a soul, not a cat.

(?)

Chapter 2

Quay of Entry-into-the-Matter

Inspector Blognard was seated at his desk which was in his office which was on Quay of Entry-into-the-Matter. You read "seated at..." and you immediately imagine the inspector seated *before* his desk, in his armchair, engaging in the customary activities of his inspectorship. You are mistaken.

Inspector Blognard was seated *behind* his desk. It is important to know the reason for this, for it sheds a light as instantaneous as it is raw upon the unorthodox methods of our inspector, our most famous unraveler of criminal enigmas.

Let us visualize the desk: the desk is placed opposite the door, between the two windows looking out on the quay. It's a desk which has a front and a back, and the front faces the door.

Stationing himself *behind* his desk, Blognard can see the quay, the river and its barges, but—and this is the crucial point—he has his back turned toward the door.

When someone enters, Blognard first perceives him *in the mirror* set in front of him on the desk. "In order to solve enigmas," he would say to Arapède, his assistant, "you must look truth in the face, in the world beyond the looking glass." "Yes, boss," Arapède would answer, with great mental reservations, for he held a philosophically skeptical vantage, and did his best to live out his skepticism, which is no simple matter. The idea of truth made him slightly seasick. But he showed no signs.

On that morning, a scant few hours after the tragic events

of the first chapter, the view over Quay of Entry-into-the-Matter was especially sublime:

—on the inspector's left, the sun was flaming red;

—the cars began to grumble continuously along the riverbank;

—a barge was lazily barging coal to somewhere or other, since no one wants coal anymore nowadays;

—there was a great hubbub over by the bridge, where firemen were struggling to free a rather ripe drowned cadaver wedged under the second pier.

The morning light entering with its familiar warmth cast itself bedazzlingly in the oval mirror set on its stand upon the desk at a slight angle.

The mirror reflected the red and dazzling sun on the one hand, the inspector's face on the other. The inspector's face was covered, along its lower half, with shaving cream. At the foot of the mirror were found a cup of very hot water, wisping its steam into the auroral air, and a small saucer with heaped mounds of dense compact cream specked with innumerable brown hairs shading toward gray.

In his hand the inspector held a "saber," an old-fashioned razor which had once belonged to Lord Bertrand Russell's barber (a gift from his old chum, Superintendent Badger, of Scotland Yard), and he was shaving, following a strict and immutable order:

a) his chin
b) his lower lip
c) his right cheek
d) his left cheek
e) his upper lip
f) his neck

It was during this shaving process in six steps (or symphonic movements) that Blognard progressed through his investigations by swift deductive insights; multiple insights were attested to, in different places, by the scars left by the razor's sharp protests.

Inspector Arapède was seated on the other side of the desk, on a chair to Blognard's left, and almost hidden by the screen of the computer terminal. He was waiting for the end of the shaving procedure and of the conversation that, simultaneously, Blognard was conducting on the telephone, to his right, with his wife Louise.

Louise Blognard was posing questions orally and dialectically, even Socratically, about the menu of their next common meal: headless larks, Pieds et Paquets, gratin Dauphinois. She successively envisaged the different hypotheses, and Blognard, in the silences following the question marks, would interject one of his ritual answers: "You think so?" "Hmm," "Yes," "No," "The one thing certain is that," "But," "Indeed," "You're right."

It was a lovers' conversation, and like lovers' conversations it ended most often without any well-drawn conclusions.

From the description we have just made, it quite evidently follows that Inspector Blognard was:

1) middle-aged;

2) in all likelihood left-handed (barring the supposition that he was, respectively: a) prematurely old; b) engaging in undignified contortions with his arms and the telephone wires).

It is important that from now on you raise the attention-level accorded my prose in order to take note of this sort of thing, for I will not always have the time, in the subsequent chapters—nor the patience—to point it out to you as we proceed along.

* * *

If the inspector found himself in his office at this very early hour in the morning, it was because they had, Arapède and he, spent the night on the premises. This often happened to them.

A bizarre and serious case had drawn to its conclusion through the confession of the guilty party, who, the very day before, was still only the number one suspect.

A precious jade vase, shaped like a *barraquet* bean, had been broken by a criminal hand in a celebrated cathedral. Very quickly, Arapède's suspicions had turned upon the most innocent, in appearance, of the witnesses: a man who sold nails, known and respected in Soissons.

The whole night long, Blognard and Arapède had taken turns at the bedside of this dark soul, so as to bring him back to the straight path, aided by a confession. In other words, they had interrogated him.

The interrogations were conducted in a small windowless room, lit by a single bare 60-watt bulb, hanging down from the white ceiling between the white walls. The floor was covered with yellow linoleum, always clean, gleaming with cleanliness (Arapède attended to this, using, as I myself [I also have a yellow linoleum floor and white walls, and a naked bulb on the ceiling], the cleaning product best suited for this task: Brilliance of Seltzer).

The suspect was seated on a plastic yellow chair, but a yellow that was hideous, jarring; the hideousness of the color and form of this chair were such that the suspect's stomach turned at the sight of it; he had only one wish: to flee from it, to feel himself no longer seated on an object of such ugliness. As the hours of the night passed, the ugliness of this chair, of this yellow clashing with the other so attractive shade of the floor, ended up by undermining the suspect's mental defenses, making him unsure of himself, left with only one dream: deliverance.

And meanwhile Blognard and Arapède paced the room in an incessant spiraloid movement. Blognard, without specifically addressing the subject, carried on out loud a monologue about the Case. He kept turning over all the circumstances, all the details, constructed all the hypotheses, recalled all the witnesses, the clues, the proofs. He did not lie to the suspect. He practiced what he called the "Strategy of Truth."

During that night, which was the last of the investigation, the one when the guilty party was going to surrender (this he knew, and the guilty man, deep down, knew it too), it was not by cunning that he advanced toward the ineluctable goal, but by absolute sincerity. In the reconstruction of the facts, he hid none of the weaknesses still noticeable in his position, but *these very weaknesses became strong points.* For the factual evidence that he *knew,* and which at any rate, sooner or later, he would be able to *prove,* appeared. So then, what good is it to keep fighting? he would kindly ask at times.

Arapède, on the other hand, during these meditative silences, read.

He read, in hushed tones and an even voice, difficult passages from a work of philosophy, commenting on it with several critically destructive interpolations. On that night, that of The Case of the Broken Vase, he had thus declaimed, hours on end, the *Etimologies* of the philosopher Orsells without ever—despite the mute, despairing questionings of the suspect, who made out the title in Arapède's hands— reading a single one of the passages explaining the reasons for this *i* in place of the *y* which the suspect, quite the nail-merchant that he was, but educated nevertheless and semi-finalist in the departmental spelling bee in Oise, knew to be found in the word *etymology.*

At six o'clock, finally, the confession came: "Yes, I'm the one who broke the vase." And, relieved, the guilty man was taken away, to be handed over to the Soissons police.

After hanging up and wiping off one last streak of cream from his face, Blognard said to Arapède: "Nothing this morning, I believe. Let's go to bed."

At that moment, the telephone rang!

It was the Big Boss.

"Is that you, Blognard?"

"Yes, it's me."

"I'm not disturbing you, I hope?"

"Not at all."

"An affair of the utmost importance and difficulty and delicacy. I have just been informed by Monsignor Fustiger himself, you see? Bla bla bla . . . bla bla bla."

Blognard was no longer listening, merely recording automatically the few details worth grasping in the stream of words at once political, confused and urbane of his superior who, as is vulgarly said, was in the process of "dumping the baby in his lap" while washing his own hands of the matter.

The message, coated with the sugar of the implied and the nougat of reasons of state, was clear: if you succeed, I pocket the media dividends; if you fail, you're to blame.

Hanging up, Blognard sat motionless a moment, staring at the glittering ball of the sun in the mirror. Then he shook his head and said: "Murder at Sainte-Gudule. Let's get over there."

And off they went.

Chapter 3

The Scene of the Crime

The victim's cadaver was discovered at 6:14 (local time) by Madame Eusèbe, grocer at 53 Rue des Citoyens.

Like every other day for the past forty-one years, after her ablutions she had gone over to Sainte-Gudule for her morning prayers. All this time she had been praying each blessed day for her sin to be pardoned. Madame Eusèbe's Sin belonged to the Distant Causes of the Immediate Causes of the events presently recounted, therefore to the Pre-Pre-History of the novel, but we are unable to say anything about it (and I am sorry). She also had been praying, but for only a few months, for the return of Alexandre Vladimirovitch, her lost, beloved cat.

On the morning in question, she had awakened in a state of joy, with an unexplainable premonition (can premonitions ever be explained? It's even harder than explaining feelings, and that's saying a mouthful) that she was going to see Alexandre Vladimirovitch again. The weather was cool and beautiful like Alexandre Vladimirovitch's fur on a spring dawn. The weather was beautiful and cool, which proved this time beyond doubt that we couldn't have been in Belgium. Hurrying off to church, Madame Eusèbe felt her burden of sin grow light.

She advanced down the central aisle toward the altar, before turning left to reach the sixth prie-dieu in the ninth row. The row was still gloomy in the faint morning light, and she thought she saw something that looked like a dark heap, over there, *in the place that had always been hers.* Her heart began to beat very hard in her old chest. She drew near.

And discovered the cadaver.

Letting out a heartrending cry, she collapsed in an unconscious heap (that makes two heaps).

Madame Eusèbe's cry as she fainted at the sight of the victim, the blood, and the victim's blood was perceived as disquieting by the pastor of Sainte-Gudule, who was reviewing his next mass in the sacristy.

This cry made his blood run cold.

He rushed into the church. At first he thought there were two cadavers, for Madame Eusèbe had fallen at the feet of the first corpse and got smeared with blood. But he saw that she was still breathing. His first thought was to telephone the police. But then he spotted, once again in the ninth row, not far from the cadaver's head, something that made him change his mind.

It was a blue chalk drawing. The spiraloid strokes composing it (see plate, page 136) imitated with mind-boggling precision the portrait of the sacred snail which reigns on the pediment of the Poldevian Chapel (as in all places of worship of the six chief denominations of Poldevia). Everyone knows that the snail is the Poldevians' totemic animal (which that country saved from total extinction from starvation during the last ice age, as attest the enormous snail fossils discovered by archaeologists at Poldevian digs [a furious controversy is raging in scientific circles on this subject: prehistoric Poldevians fed on snails, certainly, but how did they cook them? *A la cargolade? A la sussarele?* Following a lost ancestral recipe? The mystery remains]). The snail of the Poldevian Chapel is twice sacred, consecrated as it was by Monsignor Fustiger himself at the time of the dedication.

The pastor's duty was imperative: inform the monsignor. There was not a moment to be lost.

When Blognard and Arapède entered Sainte-Gudule, the place was swirling with activity.

Madame Eusèbe was being held up by a detachment of

neighbors and colleagues, who lavished her with comforting words and horrific hypotheses likely to plunge her back into unconsciousness.

At the same time, the solemn-looking pastor was chatting with the archbishop's envoy, the personal adviser to Monsignor Fustiger; he also had a look that was solemn, but equally diplomatic.

In a corner, the two bell ringers Molinet Jean and Crétin Guillaume were patiently awaiting the approach of the next hour, without suspecting the role they had played in the drama. To pass the time, they recited under their breath, faster and faster: "Since six saws saw six cigars, do six hundred six saws saw six hundred six cigars?" The answer: "Yes"; then, you say: "If six to the sixth saws saw six to the sixth six cigars, how many cigars do six to the sixth to the sixth to the sixth six saws saw?" It's a fascinating game.

A few onlookers, among whom a group of tourists, half Japanese and half Poldevian, struggled to get a glimpse of the victim who was, despite his (yes, I did say *his*) reservations, getting photographed from every angle. When the two inspectors entered, a quiver of interest passed through the crowd. People recognized Blognard.

Someone was kneeling by the cadaver: the forensic surgeon, Doctor Petiot. Spotting Blognard, he got up and extended a hand all splotched and burned with acids (in his idle moments he engaged in very precise experiments concerning the dissolution of animal flesh in different acids: smoking nitric, sulfuric, hydrochloric, not to mention citric and formic, with a view to writing a major study on the question). Dispensing with the usual courtesies, he said:

"Time of death: midnight, give or take two hours.

"Cause of death: a blunt instrument at the base of the skull; fractured cranium, et cetera.

"Victim: masculine sex.

"Age: middle, a layman's opinion, it's not really my line.

19

"No marks of appendicitis.

"Autopsy report: in my hands in forty-eight hours.

"No questions?

"He's all yours."

.   .   .

Blognard looked at the body. He stared at it intensely, with all the intensity, all the penetration he was able to muster. For Blognard this first moment of inspection held the same importance as the first glance between lovers. It marked the beginning of a mutual involvement with one thing at stake: the secret of the deceased—the name of Blognard's rival, the criminal. He and the victim had to become acquainted as intimately as possible. And the victim would be evasive, elusive, try to defend this secret: his or her life. But Blognard would need to overcome his reservations. In the victim's past, which was the future of their relationship, something, somewhere at some moment had initiated, as they say in computer language, the inexorable program that was going to lead to death, to murder. In the victim's life, as on a video cassette played backwards, the unknown face would appear, the murderer's very own.

That was why Blognard was looking so intensely at the body. He had understood right away that it would be especially difficult.

This dead body was not like just any body. He and the body did not quite speak the same language. It belonged to a familiar world, certainly, but one to which Blognard, by his makeup, could not gain easy entry. During the investigation this time he would not be able, without enormous effort, to think like his victim, to reason like him. (This was Blognard's claim to originality: the majority of history's great detectives strive to think like the criminal, to put themselves in his place; a grievous error! The victim is the one who has the

decisive role in the crime; the criminal is merely his shadow.)
He experienced a momentary panic: and if the criminal also ...
But he got hold of himself at once: no doubt exhaustion, insomnia, the letdown after solving The Case of the Broken Vase.
Looking away from the cadaver, henceforth indelibly
photographed upon his memory (and upon the negatives of
the Criminal Records Office), he slowly circled the scene of
the crime with his gaze. How had the dead body gotten here?
By its own means? Why here, in this place? The crowd of
questions crushed against him.

And, as a matter of fact, his eyes fell upon those of a
woman in the crowd, a seated old woman, surrounded by
other women consoling her, questioning her, drinking in her
words, studying her admiringly and greedily. (It is none
other, as we know, than Madame Eusèbe.) It happened like
lightning, almost at once gone dark again, an electrical
current between them. That old woman *knew* something. Or
rather, Blognard told himself, she was afraid of something.
She was afraid of something that she was *afraid of knowing.*

Let us try to keep a little ahead of the inspector. The
wretched fellow moves so quickly. Fortunately, we have our
own sources. We were practically present at the murder.

We ourselves *know* that the victim was scared of Alexandre
Vladimirovitch. We have known that from chapter 1 and we
have not already forgotten it. In addition we know that
Madame Eusèbe had had a premonition: she was going to see
once more her lost, beloved cat, Alexandre Vladimirovitch.
Thus we are able, with the help of Blognard's bolt of intuition,
to guess what Madame Eusèbe so dreads: that Alexandre Vladimirovitch, having come back to the City, is *implicated* in the
murder. This thought gives her no peace. Her sin slips her mind,
for the pardon of which on this day she has not yet prayed.

Blognard has no time to linger long over his intuition, nor
to begin verifying it. There was a sort of din in the church; all

eyes turned toward the entrance.

Père Sinouls had just arrived, accompanied by the morbid curiosity and deliciously pleased pity of those present. He moved forward bowed by emotional pain complicated by physical pain (the latter was due to gout: he had a violent attack of gout, due to neglect and beer). Leaning on the arms of two young women, he had just recognized the victim.

A neighbor, Madame Yvonne, the owner of the Gudule Bar, had awakened him to announce, as delicately as possible, the terrible news. He had been in the middle of a recurrent and troublesome dream: the master André Isoir was severely criticizing the way he had played one of Pachelbel's chaconnes on the organ, which nevertheless he was convinced he had executed with an expert touch.

He had not wanted to come alone; his daughters being gone, he had called upon two young women who now were supporting him down the center aisle of Sainte-Gudule. The one holding him up on the right was a redhead. Her name was Laurie. We will get back to her shortly.

The other, holding up Père Sinouls's left side, is the Beautiful Heroine of the novel: Hortense. The time has not yet arrived to describe her to you, for Père Sinouls has reached the ninth row. Arapède and Blognard move to the side. Père Sinouls moves forward by himself up to the sixth prie-dieu. He looks at the dead body.

The terror is still evident in his features, but they are at the same time somewhat softened, stamped with the noble serenity preceding the final dissolution. At peace. He will suffer no more; he will no longer be hungry, or thirsty, he will no longer undergo love's torments.

In one last defensive gesture, at the moment of the fatal blow, he pulled in his tail between his back paws. His fur is soaked with blood.

"Ah, poor old boy!" said Sinouls.

The victim is his dog, Balbastre.

Chapter 4

Hortense

Hortense is the heroine; she is not simply a heroine but *the* Heroine. And she's a Beautiful Heroine: *the* Beautiful Hortense.

What's more, she is My Own Personal Heroine. I who am the Author of this novel draw confidence in my undertaking from the fact that I have a beautiful heroine to offer my readers. It strikes me (but perhaps I'm mistaken) that having before one's eyes, at least while reading, a beautiful heroine, someone friendly and not imbecilic, should be cause for encouragement, given the general difficulty of existence. In the fundamental debate animating literature from its very inception—is it better to have a young beautiful friendly heroine, in good health, or an old ugly odious ailing hero—I staunchly align myself with the first position.

Hortense, therefore, is the Heroine. And yet here, today, I cannot paint her portrait.

The reason is simple: my Publisher has forbidden me to do so.

And why does my Publisher forbid me to paint Hortense's portrait, my beautiful heroine, who has all the physical and mental attributes of a young and beautiful heroine? Well now, it's precisely *because of her physical attributes*, upon which, in the first typewritten version of my Opus, I proved inexhaustible.

It so happens that my Publisher is presently practicing self-censorship. In the world, from which I keep my distance, dissatisfied with its ways, and punishing it by my absence

23

for not conducting itself in a manner more to my liking, in the world, I repeat, publishers presently possess two rather fierce enemies: according to mine, who grumbled the names over the phone (*grumble* is one of those old words designating the tone a publisher uses when asking an author to make cuts), a certain Q-isn't-that-so and a certain Reckless Disregard (such is what I made out under his grumbling, complicated by a diplomatic cough) have something against the physical attributes of heroines (and people say it is far worse for heroes).

I said to my Publisher: "I don't see why, since these Misters Q-isn't-that-so and Reckless Disregard are stricken with Stunted Tomato Bush virus, Tobacco Necrosis virus, not to mention probably Pleated Turnip virus (these three genuine viruses have obligingly been furnished to me by Julie Sinouls), I don't see, I say (I said), why I cannot expatiate on my heroine's physical attributes, details expected by my readers, and especially on that distinctive feature, one of exceptional charm, possessed by a certain lower intermediate and retroposed part of her person, at once so rare and so moving?"

He didn't want to hear another word about it.

Yet I know Hortense very well. I know her in her every detail, lengthwise and widthwise, frontwards and backwards, from top to bottom, with the best and most honorable intentions naturally, that is in my capacity as Author. I have very often been obliged, as a result of my pressing needs in preparing and imagining my tale, to follow her into her bed, into one of those long bubble baths abubble with balsamic suds, or under cold exhilarating showers that draw up on end the points atop those twin hemispheres lower than her neck. I saw her in the rain, in the warm sea at midnight, in the summer upon cool grass; and, in each one of these circumstances, her clothes were situated at some distance from her.

I explained all this to my Publisher, but he remained adamant.

I met Hortense in the T-line bus during the period when, a young philosophy major and disciple of our great philosopher Philibert Orsells, she would go over, diligent and studious, to the Library of our City to engage in the orgy of reading necessary for preparing her thesis (since completed): *On Some of the Disconcerting but Inescapable Implications of the Fundamental Principle of Onthetics.* I myself frequented the Library back then. We often met each other. I mean that our paths often coincided on the same T-bus, the narrow, complex but chaste relationship of an Author and his Heroine not permitting anything other than an invisible coincidence: a novel is not an autobiography.

And such is how, one day, not far from me, a young man dressed in black sat down across from her and uttered a sentence that was the beginning of an intense lovers' adventure between them.

So you do understand that my relationship with Hortense wasn't born yesterday.

Let us recap what needs to be known, for the moment, about Hortense's past adventures:

1) meeting the young man;

2) Hortense was in love, Hortense was suspicious, Hortense was betrayed (but not lovingly), Hortense stopped being in love, for the young man had betrayed and disappointed her;

3) Regardless, she kept taking the T-bus to get to the Library and to courageously persevere in whipping up her thesis;

4) Meanwhile there was a cat, whose name was Alexandre Vladimirovitch. He was a dashing cat, a hero. A Dashing Cat Hero. He was loved by Madame Eusèbe. He fell in love with a ginger cat, a lovely little ginger cat, called Tioutcha;

5) Meanwhile there was a criminal, tracked by Inspector Blognard and his faithful assistant, Inspector Arapède;

6) All these events of the past, all these adventures, criminal and/or amorous, possessed more or less as a center of gravity and barycenter the vicinity of Sainte-Gudule, with its Poldevian Chapel, and its square, Square des Grands-Edredons (see plate, page 135);

7) Meanwhile Inspector Blognard reached the end of his investigation and named a culprit, who was arrested;

8) Alexandre Vladimirovitch and a Poldevian prince, Prince Gormanskoï, disappeared the same day;

9) Madame Eusèbe was inconsolable; Balbastre, Père Sinouls's dog, was relieved;

10) Time passed;

11) Time passed so well that it soon was that spring night when the poor devil Balbastre got murdered.

* * *

It has often been remarked upon that all things are in everything inextricably entwined. As far as the present goes, it is steeped in the past like a fly in jam. That is why these fragments of Hortense's past are necessary to comprehend her present, the present of this narrative which is our concern.

We notice however that Hortense, who is leading and supporting Père Sinouls on his left side, is preoccupied.

Laurie notices this too.

Yet only with difficulty can this concern be attributed to Balbastre's death, terribly tragic as it may be, and to Père Sinouls's subsequent grief. Père Sinouls will get over it. The relationship between Hortense and Balbastre had never been very close, even if the latter attempted at times with his muzzle to explore those parts of Hortense's body I am forbidden to describe.

We are convinced it involves something else.

Laurie thinks so too. Let's follow them.

26

Having seen Père Sinouls back to his garden, having softened him up a bit with a few reminiscences and mental tickles along with cool beer, Hortense and Laurie took leave and went over to the Gudule Bar. Laurie ordered coffee with a glass of water from the Handsome Young Man who was Madame Yvonne's new waiter; Hortense had coffee and cream, with no glass of water, but with bread and butter.

"Feel better now?" Laurie said.

"No," said Hortense.

You must be told that Hortense was married.

This is how it came about: after having been in love and more in love, Hortense was sad; being sad, she had allowed herself to be a little in love with a man who had presented himself to her as a mainstay and consolation.

She had thrown herself into philosophic work.   X

Her consoler and mainstay was named Georges Mornacier; he was a journalist and narrator: a reporter at the City *Newspaper*, where he was assigned to follow the investigations of Inspector Blognard, whose scribe and biographer he became. He was a narrator (the character who says "I" and recounts) in the novel I had written where I told of Hortense's adventures, how she had fallen in love with her Handsome Young Man, how and why she had stopped loving him, and how she had then met Monsieur Mornacier, a journalist who precisely was the Narrator of the novel in which Hortense . . . are you following me?

They got married.

In the beginning, it wasn't so bad. Her husband was very much in love with her, she let herself go with a certain grateful kindness, even if it was not quite with the same regional bodily enthusiasms (I am proceeding with caution due to my Publisher's self-censorship) as beforehand; but come on now, marriage is marriage!

However, imperceptibly, the situation deteriorated. On the one hand, Hortense's gymnastic ardors dropped off more

and more; less and less often did she feel like playing dolls...
On the other hand, her husband's attentions and solicita-
tions, which had initially appeared to be pleasant proofs of
his interest in her person, began to weary her.

"Where are you going, my love?" he would say to her;
"What time will you be home, my love?" he would say; "Who
was that you were speaking with, my dear love, at 11:34 in
the W-line bus, between the Casanova and Cléo de Mérode
stops, darling?"

It is indeed clear that if the following expressions—"my
love," "my love," "my dear love," and "darling"—were to be
removed from the preceding statements, something like this
remains: "Where are you going? Who are you talking to?
What time are you getting home?"

A little afterwards, Hortense noticed that her husband
would watch her with a weird expression. He looked absent-
minded. He looked preoccupied, in a bad mood. He hardly
ate a thing. He ate nervously, rolling his crumbs into little
balls and cutting up his tangerine skins into 365 pieces (366,
at times). He came home from the *Newspaper* suddenly in
the afternoon after announcing that he would have to work
late into the evening. He telephoned at midnight when he
was away in the provinces trailing Blognard on a story.
Hortense didn't understand what was going on.

One day, a short while after meeting Laurie—they had
become fast friends and could talk to each other—she told
her about her confusion.

It was in the Gudule Bar. Laurie was drinking two cups of
coffee with a glass of water for each (it was noon and she was
almost awake). Hortense was having hot milk with bread
and butter. Laurie finished off her second lukewarm coffee
in one gulp, took a sip of cold water, lit a cigarette with a
match that she put back in the box with the others (the lit
and the unlit), looked at Hortense and said: "Not the slightest
clue?"

Hortense: No.

Laurie: You really want me to tell you?

Hortense: Yes, yes, things aren't right but I don't understand anything.

Laurie: Well, your old man's going bonkers.

Hortense opened her eyes (very beautiful, soft, a little blurry, large and astonished) brimming with a philosophy major's ingenuousness and lack of comprehension.

Hortense: What?

Laurie: The guy's jealous!

And by the morning of the murder, things still hadn't been set right, quite the contrary.

Chapter 5

The Geometry Lesson

The scene shifts once again.

Leaving the scene of the crime, we went out of Sainte-Gudule behind Père Sinouls, still supported by Hortense and Laurie, we crossed Rue des Grands-Edredons, we led Père Sinouls as far as his restful garden, a welcome spot for consolation, then we came over to wait for Hortense and Laurie at the Gudule Bar. Peacefully, we drink: I a Canada Dry, as usual, and you, Reader, a what-have-you, it's up to you. We look out of the Gudule Bar window, between the green plants, and we see someone coming out of the church and heading with determination toward the square near Grands-Edredons.

Who is it?

Me.

Yes, me the Author of this book.

Some smart aleck once wrote: "You cannot stand in the window and watch yourself passing by in the street." Nevertheless this is what we are now doing. I am in the street and you, my Reader, you are walking along at my side. And at the same time, I am in the Gudule Bar, still with you, two tables away from Hortense and Laurie, who do not notice us:

a) because they are absorbed in their own conversation and their eye-conversation with the Handsome Young Man who just started waiting tables at the Gudule Bar (he wasn't here the last time, that they're sure of);

b) because we are invisible and conceptual.

But be careful, there is "we" and "we." Or more precisely,

there is "me" and "me" (as far as you're concerned, things are even more complicated, and I'll let you get yourself out of the topological and existential implications of your situation).

Let us call, if you like, me-1 the person (me) who is in the Gudule Bar. Me-1 looks and explains what is going on. This is the inalienable right and sacred duty of the Narrator: to look at what happens and relate it accordingly to the Reader. But you will readily admit that at times there is something just a wee bit disappointing, even exasperating, in this purely passive role of invisible voyeur who can't get a word in, who can't act in any way whatsoever.

This is where Me-2 comes in. Me-2 is still me, the Author, but a "me" directly entering into the story, a "me" made of flesh and blood as much as of eye and thought. I bask in the sunlight which in the morning brightens the house and shop fronts along Rue des Grands-Edredons, the Gudule Bar, the corner of Rue des Milleguiettes where we were last night, the Grocery Theater which just opened on the corner of Rue Vieille-des-Archives (the excellent plays put on in the Grocery Theater—the audience sits on crates of concentrated milk—all possess an inevitable connection with the place: *The Adventures of an Oleaginous Plant; The Carrot Who Wanted to Grow in Sand; The Memoirs of a Cheeky Eggplant*), whereas the facade of 53 Rue des Citoyens (where I am heading), on the side of the square, is still in the shade.

I enter this house. I am going to have my geometry lesson.

The door of D stairway was open and at the bottom of the steps I met Carlotta. She was wrapped up in conversation with her girlfriend Eugénie.

On that morning, Carlotta was 15 80/365 years old. She was a redhead and was temporarily five feet five inches tall (in rapid transition toward sixteen years old and five feet six inches). Eugénie was blond and needed one hundred fifty-five days and one inch to catch up with Carlotta (her attitude showed that she did not have, for the moment, any great hope of making up the one hundred and fifty-five days). Eugénie lived on the fourth floor of A stairway.

Now Carlotta had been for several days theoretically deprived of Eugénie's company and Eugénie of Carlotta's. This was the result of a Decree of Madame Eugénie, who had had an academic difference with her daughter and wished to inspire her to show more concentration. They were not allowed to pay each other the thirty-seven daily visits and the sixty-three telephone calls indispensable to their friendship (and Madame Eugénie, it must be said, would really have liked to be able to have use of her own phone). Thus they met at the bottom of stairways A and D, alternately. You could be practically certain of finding them, outside of school hours, in one of these two places.

"Ciao," said Eugénie upon spotting me, for it was time for my lesson.

Wishing to keep myself abreast of the latest developments in modern science, which is absolutely indispensable in our day and age for an Author, I recently became aware of my absolute ignorance of geometry. As Père Sinouls obligingly explained to me, with supporting examples drawn from Edward Nelson's predicative arithmetic, from lambda-calculus ("which is not calculus-lambda," he had interjected with a laugh), not to mention Bénabou-style fibered categories, I was, through my ignorance, practically ill-equipped for:

1) computer programming;

2) the in-depth comprehension of the mechanisms of our "beautiful society" (the " " should be understood, in the Sinoulsian idiom, as quotation marks both exclamatory and sarcastic).

I shyly asked him for a little catch-up course. He had the kindness to rapidly sketch out for me one of the hundred and one first demonstrations of Pappus's theorem on the corner of a Social Security form, but he cut off abruptly, citing his gout, his ontological problems and his tennis elbow. He advised me to seek out Carlotta, presently a tenth-grader at the lycée Faraday. "She's Laurie's daughter," he told me, "Hortense's new friend."

Things are becoming clear, aren't they? Carlotta is Laurie's daughter; Laurie is Hortense's friend; Hortense, the heroine, is a friend of Père Sinouls; Père Sinouls is an old friend of the Author. They belong to the same generation, they have passed through the same ordeals. I am going to have my geometry lesson.

In actual fact, put your mind at ease, dear Reader; you yourself don't need to take geometry lessons. All you will need to do is attend, as a spectator, the one that will be unfolding before your eyes. Geometry is not absolutely indispensable for catching on to the basic elements of this story. Let us say that it provides us an excellent excuse to get inside the fourth-floor apartment, on the right, D stairway, at 53 Rue des Citoyens. And that's something really necessary.

*   *   *

I entered with infinite precaution (I had excellent reasons for being cautious). I came to a branching entrance-hallway irrigating the four rooms and annexes of the apartment. On the right of the straight corridor: the kitchen; on the left: the main room for eye (television), ear (stereo blaster), and mind (shelved books). (Plus a sofa for sleeping annexishly and a rocker for rocking while singing one of Jane Birkin's songs.) Opposite the entrance: the bathroom; on the right: Carlotta's room. On the left, the branch of the hallway leading, to its right, to the "place of tranquil retreat and reading far from the anguish of the floating world" (also containing Hotello's litterbox and *Crossword Puzzles* by Georges Perec); straight ahead, at last, to the room of Carlotta's mother, Laurie.

The kitchen and Carlotta's bedroom both looked out upon

the intersection of Rue des Citoyens and Rue Vieille-des-Archives where, thanks to the acerbic comments contained in my first novel, the city had finally decided to install a traffic light, thus decreasing by 83 percent the amount and intensity of sheet metal rumbling, pedestrian rustling and altercations between motorists (much to the despair of the ornithologists who, following the extinction of most species, made the transition to collecting bird *names*).

Mornings, the Sun, upon rising, came for breakfast in the spacious, comfortable kitchen. Raising the shutter, he easily slipped his beams through the pane without either twisting or damaging them, cast a glance upon the red memorandum where he read (with slight indiscretion) the latest exchanges between Carlotta, Laurie, and Hotello, looked absentmindedly at the ceiling, and then slowly headed for the hallway. (The Sun is never in a hurry, he moves forward majestically, inexorably.) How could the Sun know that the ceiling was the ceiling? plain and simply because Laurie had for his benefit beautifully inscribed precise directions, embellished with arrows. The ceiling direction was indicated by *ceiling;* likewise, the cold water faucet was labeled *cold water* and the hot water faucet *hot water;* thus, for the Sun, in this apartment, there were no unwelcome surprises. Above the kitchen table, on the wall: a map of the neighborhood, drawn house by house, allowing him to verify that he was indeed where he thought himself to be: "You are here" was written in red.

Let us leave the Sun in the kitchen and meet him again in Carlotta's room where he is simultaneously advancing (miracle of light, whose geometrical explanation is highly instructive).

Upon entering Carlotta's room, I was seriously disoriented, for the arrangement had changed in every little detail since my last geometry lesson only a week ago. Carlotta, indeed, would reorganize her room from top to bottom every six days on the average, a reorganizational operation which gave me an idea of the infinity obtained by finite means, for the result was never the same way twice. It wasn't only the bed, the desk, the chair, the lamp, the armoire, and the shelves which changed place or appearance, but also the posters, illustrations and photographs, whose layout and nature varied, a result of the hierarchical fluctuations indicating Carlotta's accelerated advance along the road leading from fifteen to sixteen. I have not forgotten the radio and television.

Cautiously I sat on a kitchen chair to the right of the desk which, that day, had its back to the door, with the window to its left. I took out my notebook for one last revision while Carlotta turned on the VCR in the main room. Hotello was stretched out casually on the desk's surface; he looked peaceful and sleepy, but his whiskers had a sort of quiver to them that did not appeal to me in the least. I did not appreciate very much his habit of using me as a target for his ambush training, nor his constant attempts to set new records in scaling my trouser legs. He climbed very quickly, of course, but he needed to get a firm hold, and it wasn't the cloth alone which suffered. In addition, needless to say, he hated geometry.

Chapter 6

Still the Geometry Lesson

All of the available surfaces in Carlotta's room, as I've said and repeat now with more details, were occupied by:
—posters,
—color photographs, chiefly human and equine, but also including koalas and kangaroos,
—self-help hints and resolutions,
—postcards sent by Laurie from different points around the globe,
—clippings, scrawlings and cutouts from newspapers, magazines, radio shows, TV...
The total ensemble was in a state of flux, perpetual mutation and variation, the layouts, arrangements and permutations charting Carlotta's ethical and aesthetic movements through the course of time. There resulted a three-dimensional work (height, width and time), a wall fresco whose ceaseless recomposition marked her accelerated progress along the arrow of time, from childhood to adolescence, and already in adolescence prefigured the unsuspected regions of her autonomous redheaded youth.

When a little more than a year beforehand I had begun, under her enlightened guidance, my study of geometry (still having trouble following her, for she reasoned and calculated more swiftly than her shadow), the dominant theme of the wall fresco was clearly equestrian: white or brown manes of bold superb horses taken from *Horse Magazine* or Stubbs's reproductions from the Victoria and Albert Museum took up nearly the whole space. But, little by little, at first diffidently,

36

then more and more swiftly, the center of gravity, the bary-center of the work, had shifted toward music. Eugénie and Carlotta had at first communed in a common and absolute love for the songs and portraits of the young men from the band Hi Hi: they were a Finlando-Poldevian band (the Poldevian grandmother of one of the fellows had settled in Helsingfors [not yet Helsinki] at the turn of the century and they publicly proclaimed these roots) whose lyrics, dis-cernible at times amid the music, caught the ear due to an indisputable syntactico-lexico-morphological originality, a working compromise between the different requirements (especially regarding word order) of Finnish, Poldevian and English; for they sang, theoretically, in English.

Here's an example: "I have my heart insidethr..." (inde-cipherable) "by yr image penetratedgangen in

"unless you with your kiss again my heart inside me d... skoï be givin' "

But Carlotta and Eugénie's intellectual communion in Hi Hi fandom did not last. For Eugénie (no doubt due to those one hundred fifty-five days she lagged behind Carlotta which she did not manage to make up) had remained im-movably fixed on Hi Hi (and her mad definite love for Martenskoï, the handsomest, cutest young man out of all the handsome, cute young men in the band), whereas Carlotta had gradually replaced them in her thoughts and on her walls (as well as in her speech) by another band, pure Britishers from Liverpool (as was shown by their big hit "No" [pronounced "naw," at the lower end of the scale; it was a typically Liverpudlian "no" which linguists claim is exclu-sively uttered by men whereas woman, according to them, say "nuo," at the upper end of the scale]). This band was called Dew-Pon Dew-Val.

Carlotta had all the Dew-Pon Dew-Val posters, all their singles and albums, all their interviews in German, Japanese or Poldevian magazines with dictionary translations done

37

line by line and word by word, squeezed out of classmates who were taking German (respectively Japanese, respectively Poldevian) as first or (at the most) second language. (She engaged in a constant comparative and philologically scathing study of these different documents so as to figure out the truth from the contradictory bits of information issuing from the young men's offhand remarks and the subsequent mistranslations, not to mention what the German, Japanese and Poldevian journalists made up.)

She also had all the videocassettes of their live appearances and interviews on the eleven music television channels. And she had, rarest of treasures, three bootleg cassettes from their early days, sent from Liverpool to Laurie by Jim Wedderburn (a birthday present).

And she was in love with Tom Butler, the Handsomest Young Man in the band. Since Eugénie was still too much of a child to grasp the intrinsic superiority of Tom Butler over Martenskoï, the Handsomest Young Man in the band Hi Hi, she was obliged to commune in Dew-Pon Dew-Val with another friend, Aurélia; and it was agreed between Aurélia and her that once Tom Butler was seduced (they would meet him on Nottingham Road where the recording studio was located, whose address was mentioned in an Italian magazine that Aurélia had bought during a vacation in Rome) it was agreed that they would share him, each for a week at a time, and that they wouldn't be jealous of each other nor for that matter of Tom Butler's fiancée whose photo was put up in a good spot on the wall. On the other hand, rival bands would be treated with all the harshness they deserved... In the kitchen before my very eyes Carlotta had torn to shreds, trampled and tossed into the garbage disposal an interview with the abominable Landau Valley who had taken the liberty to make a disparaging remark about Dew-Pon Dew-Val's ultrasimplistic and relentlessly binary rhythmic line (it was afterwards proved to be pure slander on the reporter's part,

Dew-Pon Dew-Val and Landau Valley being in fact the best friends in the world, what with Tim Butler [not to be confused with Tom Butler], the second star of Dew-Pon Dew-Val, having been one of the original members of Landau Valley, plus the fact both groups used the same recording studio).

*   *   *

While humming Dew-Pon Dew-Val's latest hit, which had just moved from twelfth to eleventh place on "Thirty-Nine Steps," the TV show that played a crucial role in the music Stock Market, Carlotta adjusted the radio's volume to the requisite loudness (another Dew-Pon Dew-Val song was coming on) while the TV reran, for the sixth time, the most important segments of the Osaka airport interview they gave before leaving on their next concert tour (Romorantin the 4th, Bedarieux the 5th, Clermont-l'Herault the 6th, Chelles the 7th, Bedford the 8th, and not Bedford the 4th, Romorantin the 5th, Chelles the 6th, Bedarieux the 7th, as Carlotta pointed out, having spotted this absurd mistake in the TV schedules). With her right hand, she held out the piece of paper on which she had drawn the figure for my day's geometry lesson (here we are!).

I seized it apprehensively (admire this stylistic subtlety of "seized"; "apprehension" from *prehendere*, "to seize"—great stuff, isn't it?): there was a frightening profusion of lines, some parallel, others not, concocting innumerable triangles and certain things that looked like parallelograms, in a variety of colors, the points of intersection in capital letters sometimes modified with and even with " (Carlotta's figures were always sketched with great elegance, which made my geometric incompetence all the more inexcusable). Alas, yes, roughly guessing, they were parallelograms, but that was precisely the point of the exercise: it had to be *proved* that these things, drawn like obvious parallelograms according to the data, were indeed parallelograms. I was foolish enough to point this out to her, and she broke off her song for just a moment to chastise me: geometry is no detective novel (Carlotta was a skilled reader of Agatha Christie's novels and she had immediately found the solution to the enigma of my first novel that no critic had unraveled), you mustn't *begin* with the conclusion in order to work back to the hypothesis; you must *demonstrate* the conclusion by *using* the hypotheses. "Do you understand?" she added, gently but firmly. My heart dropped several inches in my breast, while my head swayed slightly in the shower of contradictory decibels entering my ears but which apparently did not affect Hotello.

For Carlotta had one phobia: she *hated,* almost as much as Dew-Pon Dew-Val's enemies Landau Valley (in fact, she *despised* those guys), she hated Thales and therefore I was not allowed to use the theorem known by the name of "Thales' theorem" in the hearts of geometry fans. Given the innumerable parallels with which the figure was cluttered in every corner, I was left with scant hope. "Figure it out," Carlotta said to me. "But no Thales." And she reran thirty-seven times on her VCR the beloved face of Tom Butler.

I tackled my task with determination; in the first place, because I did not wish to lose too much esteem in Carlotta's harsh but fair eyes; in the second, because I had the hope, if I properly carried out my parallelogramatic proof, of receiving her enlightened help for a project that I had recently formed, and for which her insights were indispensable—but I'll speak of this project in its own time and place.

Hotello had moved away from the desk, having failed, under Carlotta's watchful eye, to make off with my pencil to his stash of booty (which essentially contained objects stolen, out of love, from Laurie and Carlotta). There was some sort of noise in the adjoining room; I hardly heard a thing because of the TV, the radio and my intense effort of concentration on the barycenter of C and of M' with the coefficients 15 and -37 respectively. Yet Carlotta's sharp ear must have registered the sound, since she abruptly left the room and shortly afterward I heard, this time distinctly, a slam and then Hotello skidding across the parquet, its whole surface agleam thanks to the amount of Brilliance de Panzer spread upon it by the surface technician; an Hotello seeking to escape punishment. His ferocious jealousy of Laurie was brought to bear upon what he considered to be rivals for his affection: green plants. As soon as he was able (and the geometry lesson struck him as a propitious moment) he did everything to give them what they deserved, scratching with his claws, scattering the soil from their pots and chewing up their leaves.

"So," Carlotta said, "how's your proof coming along?"

Part Two

The Poldevian Connection

Chapter 7

Hotello and Laurie

Hotello had shown up a few months before at Laurie and Carlotta's place. He had scratched at the third floor right on D stairway. He explained that it had come to his attention there was a vacancy for a cat in this apartment.

Indeed, a few weeks earlier, Laurie's cat, Liiliii, the most stylish cat of its generation who, with a shrug of its gray shoulders accompanied by an imperceptible sway of its tail, knew how to express an entire universe of feelings, had stupidly allowed herself to be kidnapped on the Square des Grands-Edredons where she was taking her daily after-lunch stroll.

This kidnapping, about which there will be much to say (for it does not belong to the Pre-Pre-History of the drama we are living, like Madame Eusèbe's Sin, but to the causes and premonitory circumstances of the events that we are presently relating), had left Laurie and Carlotta in pain, sorrow, cold fury and disarray. They came up empty-handed at every turn. Yet they had a description of the Kidnapper, and her (apparently it was a "her") Identikit picture had been posted everywhere in the neighborhood, along with a beautiful color photo of Liiliii. Laurie and Carlotta had received dozens of calls. They were offered: eleven female cats, brown, yellow or black; three dogs: a briard and two cocker spaniels; a bicycle; four marriage proposals. Liiliii had been spotted buying a high-speed train ticket for Lyon-Perrache; coming out of a Cabinet meeting; reading *A Guide to Small-scale Goatbreeding* (in English, published by the Overlook Press) . . .

After Cordelia James, the private eye they had hired as a last resort, failed, Laurie and Carlotta acknowledged:

—that for the moment there was no hope of finding Liiliii again;

—that the thought of getting their lives back together with another cat who would never be as stylish was out of the question;

—that it was also out of the question to remain without a feline (the reason will be given a little later).

Since Laurie ruled out Carlotta's idea of a delightful baby panther, they resigned themselves to considering a male cat.

The day following this decision, Hotello showed up. Please make note of this fact and, to impress it upon your attention, I emphatically repeat:

The day following this decision, Hotello showed up.

He said he was a year old; that he never knew his parents; that his fur was black and he had no special markings.

In fact, his coat was a bright, beautiful, lustrous black, shiny and supple, almost too beautiful, almost too perfect.

He had remained rather evasive about his place of origin and his life before coming into the house. He had only mumbled something vague about a park, an orphanage. But Carlotta and Laurie had respected his reluctance to speak, not being inquisitorial by nature nor themselves unduly prone to confidences. After all, that was his business. He wanted to be a cat at 53 Rue des Citoyens, third door on the right. OK, they needed a cat; and a cat he was. They could always give it a try and see what would happen.

The question that now comes up is: why is a cat, male or female, necessary in this apartment where there are already horse posters, two radios, two Walkmans, a stereo blaster, two TVs, a VCR jointly owned by mother and daughter, not to mention the ficus and other green plants and the sunshine which enters in the morning through the kitchen window and leaves at night by the square before settling

46

down in the hollow of Sainte-Gudule's shoulder? For what it's worth, I shall reveal my own interpretation, which requires a few remarks of the preliminary sort.

* * *

A few years after the turn of the century which is now drawing to its close, if I can go by what I read in the papers, a redheaded Irishman named Bloom came to settle somewhere in the right haunch of our country, in the between-two-counties overlooking the river which then flows down to the sea; the name of the one is contained in the name of the other, a clue which will suffice, I think, to identify them. Several decades later, a girl was born, with red hair and the name Laurie Bloom (you're caught up short in your protests, you thought I was going to tell you the whole family history); this little girl, remaining so for only the requisite years, growing up in turn became the mother of Carlotta. Laurie, like her Irish grandfather, was redheaded, and so was Carlotta.

Dorothy Edwards at one time made a judicious remark that I quote from memory, roughly: "There is something intrinsically delightful in a female redhead's skeleton. If one day you must have a conversation with a ghost, it would be pleasanter to have it with the ghost of a female redhead." This is quite true. But it must be added that female redheads' skeletons possess one special feature; they are, not any less intrinsically, charged with an immense, inexhaustible amount of static electricity.

Perhaps you don't know what static electricity is. I recommend the following experiment: one very cold day, try to touch the metal knob of a door in a motel room by the shores of the Mississippi (in Prairie-du-Chien, for example); you will understand, with the radiating, unexpected shock that spreads up to your shoulder across your elbow, what the discharge of a sizable quantity of static electricity is. Now, a

47

female redhead contains at all times a hundred times higher dose of electricity stored up in her delightful skeleton. If you brush against her, I don't mean physically but verbally and with no precautions, the electrocuting reaction is so strong and so swift that it will plaster you on the ceiling. Unless, as in Laurie's case, a safety mechanism for the protection of others does not redirect the electrical current inward; but then, she is the one plastered on the ceiling, which is not much of an improvement.

Now imagine what might result from the coincidence in the same apartment of *two* female redheads, who furthermore share a fair amount of their genetic patrimony since one is the daughter of the other and the other is the mother of the first. You grasp the problem.

What's the solution? It's very simple. A cat is needed. A cat has its own dose of mental and nervous electricity, and it is cut out to play the role of the third pole in this electromagnetic system that old Maxwell had not foreseen. Cats understand redheaded women to perfection; black male cats especially, because of their color contrast with the principal bipole, both feminine and red.

It so strikes me that herein lies the reason Hotello's application was welcomed, despite certain strange obscure points in his story which, upon being presented to me, I recorded deep in my Hertz of hearts. Hotello must have sensed my suspicions for he did not display an automatic hostility toward me but rather a silent disdain; and he did everything to terrorize me by surprise leaps on my shoulders from the tops of armoires or the highest bookshelves, or else from underneath armchairs, bloodying my calves. In this he was perfectly successful.

Coming there to live, he had had in mind an obscure but deeply rooted idea. He was not one to lead a retiring life. His bearing clearly showed that he was used to commanding, to doing as he pleased, but here things weren't working out.

Each time he'd get yelled at, he'd put on a stubborn look, dropping his ears, and whipping his tail at a frequency of once every 3.7 seconds. Then he'd relaunch his attack upon Carlotta's tender flesh, and he'd get one colossal slap. He'd slink off, temporarily ceding territory, but the thought remained all the more firmly in place.

For my part, I continued my visits despite the dangers I risked with Hotello's unpredictable ambushes. First off, my knowledge of geometry had to progress at all costs. Secondly, although Laurie and Carlotta did not seem to be aware of Hotello's secret ploy, I was intrigued by it. Of course I know (since I am engaged in writing this novel, I therefore know everything) what Hotello's objective had been in moving into these premises.

Finally, one other reason guided my steps across the Square des Grands-Edredons: I was taking mental notes for my *Treatise on Comparative Redheadedness*, which I had begun by studying Armance, the oldest of the Sinouls girls. The first time Père Sinouls came to Laurie's, he triggered such an electrical reaction from Carlotta that he left exhausted, confessing to me that only then did he understand to what degree his daughter Armance had mellowed; he felt like he had been thrown backwards eight years to the time when Armance was fourteen.

Chapter 8

The Poldevian Chapel

There were several anomalies in Hotello's autobiographical pronouncements, several curious features to his behavior. Here I will draw attention to three facts.

In the first place, it was curious that he showed up at the apartment the very day after Laurie's and Carlotta's decision to take on a cat as a resident, while waiting for Liiliii to come back. They hadn't yet mentioned it to *anybody*. Hotello's unexpected arrival struck them as coincidental. But I had my doubts. Coincidence is the novelist's mortal enemy. If a novelist possesses something exclusively his own, it is surely an absolute power over events (provided they remain in a Possible Novelistic World, which constitutes the whole difficulty and the honor of our Art, its heroism in fact; we need this power, even if it is merely a power on paper, for the Real World treats us rudely, as will be seen in the next chapter). Therefore events must conform to a preestablished plan and have their explanation; explaining Hotello's arrival by the fact that he was passing by at precisely the moment when those two hyper(red) redheaded girls just happened to want a cat is a bit much!

Secondly, Hotello had come as a black cat, and in point of fact, the blackness of his coat was unbeatable. Yet one day, one freezing day, I was waiting on the sofa in the big room for my geometry lesson to start; it could not begin until Carlotta had finished the thirty-seven dangerous leaps she had set about performing both to get her intellectual juices flowing and to vent a portion of the energetic enthusiasm inspired by the purchase, the day before, of a rare poster of Dew-Pon Dew-Val in space suits. Hotello, perhaps intimidated by the dangerous leaps, or mellowed by the temperature which wasn't (mellow), had come over, an exceptional occurrence, to sit on my lap. He was purring. And while I was petting his belly, what do I discover to my great surprise but that the roots of his fur were not coal black but gray-black with a hint of blue. Hotello darted me a quick glance, immediately masked with purring, leaped nimbly from my lap and didn't climb back for at least three weeks; and that time, his fur was black to the very tips of his nails, if I dare express myself thus.

In the last place, there is something far more serious: getting home from school one afternoon an hour earlier than usual as a result of the unwitting mistake of the history teacher who had been persuaded, thanks to one of Carlotta's crafty ploys, that it was an hour later than it actually was (she was still laughing about this two months later), she (Carlotta) did not see Hotello. She called him, went around the apartment, looked in every possible cranny: nothing. A little anxious, she leaned out of the window, glanced toward the square, called again: nothing. She was already seeing him fallen from the window, hurt perhaps, crawling under a bush, unable to call out or ask for help. Laurie, questioned on the phone at her headquarters, the café L'Impérial Sentier qui Bifurque, where she was drinking her usual afternoon draft Guinness, said that when she left, Hotello was indeed there, and that she had not let him out.

However, fifty minutes later, after a fruitless search around the neighborhood, Carlotta and Laurie returned to find Hotello in the kitchen. Questioned, he claimed he had fallen asleep in the cabinet above the garbage disposal, where Carlotta was nevertheless sure she had looked. The mystery was never solved, but I did not fail to notice (without mentioning it) that he had reappeared precisely at the time when

Carlotta would have *normally gotten home from classes.*

I let you draw your own conclusions from these three facts.

In my view one thing was certain: Hotello was certainly not the little one-year-old cat, so mature for his age, that he pretended to be.

· · ·

At approximately the same time that Hotello came to live in Laurie's and Carlotta's place, I don't know if it was a little before or after (these details have no bearing on the story), the apartment behind the third door on the left C stairway at number 53 was once again occupied. I know because I'm the Author and I know everything, and you know because I'm telling you.

I can't make you witness the scene because that would require us to perform some rather pointless, inelegant spatio-temporal contortions. Let's bear in mind that we are in the Gudule Bar beside Laurie and Hortense while we are also attending my geometry lesson. That's quite a feat in itself. Take my word and my story for it.

The apartment in question had been empty for quite a while, since the day after the dedication of the Poldevian Chapel and the christening of Rue de l'Abbé-Migne by Monsignor Fustiger. On that day, when Alexandre Vladimirovitch disappeared, leaving Madame Eusèbe so inconsolably gloom-ridden (although not a widow since Eusebe, her husband, was very much alive), a moving van had come to take away the indistinct ensemble of furniture and belongings it held: indistinct because the boxes were hermetically sealed, and ensemble because I tell you so. And now once again there was someone in the apartment. A moving van came to deliver an indistinct ensemble of furniture and belongings in hermetically sealed boxes. The new owner(?) or tenant(?) of the premises yielded the room to the rough and powerful movers after having encouraged them in their chore by making some conversational remarks: "It's a nice day," said the new occupant of the third door on the left C stairway to the movers, "but there's a chill in the air." And the movers commented in chorus: "Ancient truths fall from the heavens / Let's hold out our red aprons." (They were old-fashioned movers.) Or else he said while offering them a coin, which proved to be gold and Poldevian: "Here, drink this to my health, my good fellows"; and the movers thanked him with a "Upon our napes and on our backs / Heave-ho, heave-ho our heavy sacks." This was more or less the only lively moment of his presence. He did not show his face to Madame Batus the new concierge, nor to Monsieur Boillault the butcher living in the building; he was seen neither at the Groichant Bakery, nor at the Gudule Bar, nor at the hardware store run by the married couple Lalamou-Belin. He received no mail, went out after sunset, as invisible as a man who walked through walls, and came home at dawn. He was, according to Madame Batus who met him two or three times at the bottom of the stairs because of the hours he (and she) kept, a rather good-looking man between twenty-seven and thirty-two years approximately, slightly taller than average, with light chestnut hair, and eyes of an uncertain color (it was dark and he did not raise his eyes toward her), a thin long nose, but outward identifying marks: none. He was extremely silent: not a sound from his apartment penetrated Laurie's, even though it was adjoining.

About the same time that Hotello arrived and the (new?) mysterious C stairway tenant (owner?) moved in, a little before or a little after or between the two (but it really doesn't matter), Carlotta and Eugénie made a major discovery.

One Saturday afternoon they were playing badminton in the square while waiting for Mr. Spock in "Star Trek" to come on television (maybe it was Super Jaimie, I'm not sure, the schedules would need to be consulted) when suddenly one particularly imperious swing of the racket by Carlotta sent the ball with its lace parachute over the gate separating the square from the little vegetable garden adjoining the Poldevian Chapel. It was an especially empty Saturday, a beautiful day, and just about everybody had gone off for the weekend; the square was almost silent and empty. So, without a moment's thought, Carlotta jumped over the gate after lithely climbing to the top. She landed in the Poldevian vegetable garden, in the lettuce patch. The silence was majestic; the snails, inhabitants of the garden, snored gently in the cool air. Carlotta didn't spot the ball right off and she signaled Eugénie to come join her and help. Carried away by its ballistic enthusiasm, the ball had followed a graceful trajectory and expired at the bottom of a small lean-to, in openwork wood, hidden from view either when looking in from the square, or from the windows of 53 or from Rue de l'Abbé-Migne, by a particular jutting section of the wall of Sainte-Gudule. Carlotta, taking great pains not to disturb the majestic slumber of the snails, drew close and . . . was struck speechless; a sound had just escaped from the lean-to, a sort of noble groan, slightly plaintive and disenchanted, intermingled with boredom and courage. At any rate, regardless of the psychological nuances that could be discerned in this sound by an analysis of the different resonant formants of its acoustic composition, it was an incontestable whinny. This was still during the period when Carlotta was completely enthralled by horses. She knew by heart all the articles in the *Encyclopedia of Horses*, subscribed to *Horse Magazine*, moved through obstacle races as easily as geometric theorems and had a fiancé, an Arabian-Anglo-Poldevian pure-blood named Rostang. Which is to say that she could recognize a whinny, even a muffled one, a mile off.

She signaled Eugénie to come closer, as silently as possible.

They pressed their eyes to the chinks between the boards and saw *a pony,* the most delightful, sad, lonely, moving Poldevian pony ever, with a thick red mane and a grayish gold coat, a specimen of the proudest, wildest, most fierce and beautiful race of ponies in the world. The pony looked at them in turn, found them friendly and displayed the utmost desire to get to know them more thoroughly. It was a reciprocal feeling. They stuffed him with lettuce (apologizing to the snails they awoke and displaced), kissed his muzzle, promised to bring him carrots and, at his insistence, some radishes as well. He informed them his name was Cyrandzoï. All three kissed once again effusively. Eugénie and Carlotta went back over the gate and immediately went up to Carlotta's room for a summit conference.

At that time, obviously, the walls of Carlotta's room were entirely dedicated to horses, Dew-Pon Dew-Val still existing in a nebulous future. But, for some time already, a polemical tension reigned between Laurie and Carlotta, on the one hand; between Madame Eusèbe and Eugénie, on the other. The subject of the theoretical divergence between mother and daughter was the same in each case; the daughter wanted a horse and the mother was against it, putting forward an awful hodgepodge of arguments, as follows: "I don't have the money" or "where would we keep it?" These arguments struck the mothers as pure and irrefutable, the daughters as petty subterfuge and dishonest excuses.

Now much to the general and simultaneous surprise of Madame Eugénie and Laurie (but they did not share their impressions with each other, thus missing an opportunity to find out more about their respective daughters), the demands for a horse, strong, repeated (Chinese water torture style) for several months on end, came to an abrupt halt and there was no more talk about it. Laurie thought that Hotello's arrival, which happened at this point, had something to do with it.

55

Madame Eugénie thought (she did think something or other but I don't really know what); but soon they didn't think about it anymore. Some while afterward, the two mothers, independently but simultaneously and respectively, noted certain diminishments in their small change and return-for-refund items, here and there and from time to time. Wise mothers that they were, they did not take much offense over it, blaming the times, their age, the circumstances increasing their daughters' needs, and they added a few things to the wardrobe, raised allowances. The small change disappearances grew less without entirely fading away.

Today I am in a position to reveal that this metallic vanishing had a noble, pressing and inescapable reason: sweets needed to be bought for the pony Cyrandzoï, their friend, to alleviate the suffering inflicted upon him by the necessity for concealment and confinement due to a mission of the highest order and far-reaching importance, whose nature he could not reveal to them, although he was absolutely dying to do so.

Now and then, at twilight, they climbed over the gate and galloped around the garden a few times. Hotello saw them and smiled beneath his whiskers.

Chapter 9

I Am Not Madame Bovary

(with an unpublished Correspondence between the Author and the Publisher)

I am an unassuming but determined author. When, at the age of fourteen, I conceived the project of a novelistic fresco spanning thirty-seven volumes, each thick, in which the totality of human (as well as animal) experience would be subsumed in a fearsome prose of genius, I did not lose my head,

no,

(I remember as if it were yesterday, even better. At any rate, in memory it's always yesterday, even worse, memory is the "now" that has passed by: it was a Wednesday and, as was my custom at the time, on the hill, in the shade of the old oak, at sunset, I had come to sit. I lingered long with my gaze over the plain, whose changing scene unfolded at my feet. Here rumbled the river with its frothing waves, etc., and in its waters . . .)

so then, I did not lose my head, and I waited. I was quite aware that I was unacquainted with life and with the novel, two essential prerequisites for my project. I showed patience; I lived; and I read. I read while living and I lived while reading (have I read more than I lived, or the opposite? this thought tortures me at times). But as a child, time passed, and I did not gain a greater acquaintance with life.

As for the novel, I was quite at a loss what to think about it. On the one hand, huge numbers kept being written; written

57

and published; they came in all languages, in all sorts of costumes and covers. Never could I pause a moment to catch my breath and come up with an exact appraisal of the ensemble of novelistic production before setting myself to the task. I had promised myself I would do so before I started (there's a real problem here, I prefer to warn those who will follow me in my career as a novelist: living and reading are things that take time. What's more, for all those years, I had to eat of course! I did everything, all jobs, led a simple life, kept far from the clamor, far from the cries of envy and vain ambitions. I even spent time in Montmartre, in its gypsum quarries, selling glass for watching eclipses).

On the other hand, the novel did not stop moving, in its form as well as its formats; and its name, far from remaining inflexible, as a great literary critic, Saul Kripke, recommends, did not stay in place. There was the novel called New; there was the anti-novel, the ex-novel novel and the post-novel; there was the lenov (the doctrinal novel), the loven, not to mention the lovne and the levno. I saw, or rather read, Paquerette d'Azur, our glory, pass from the literary forefronts to the storefronts, and Odilon Joyaux back to the first front without even seeming to do so. And the whole while, where was I? Nowhere, I must confess.

One morning I got up and said to myself: you know nothing, nothing, nothing; you are worthless, worthless, worthless. But is that any reason not to write a novel? Obviously not. So I took the bull by the horns. I opened a package of Buro Plus extra-strong 80 gram-weight paper (my machine spurns the other sorts). I took a sheet from the stack, I put it into my machine, a Brother CE-50, and I waited.

I waited for it to come and, when it did, I typed just as it came. Fine.

I needed, inevitably, a heroine. I chose Hortense.

I knew I had no imagination. No matter: I'll tell, I decided, only the truth. I'll simply tell about things as they had happened while happening (that's how, I don't know if your observation matches mine, things do happen). I'll set forth the events almost dryly, rinsing them of all extraneous motivations and extrinsic explanations. I will write only: there was this; there was this because there was that; first there was this, then that, then that . . . As soon as I would have told everything, a novel would come to be. I would bring it to a publisher, and that would be that.

How naïve I was, at my age (I was in my fifty-third year when my novel appeared). I'm going to tell you just how. But first of all, be careful: *I am not Madame Bovary!*

In other words, my beautiful heroine Hortense is not Madame Bovary, I am not my beautiful heroine Hortense, and it follows that I am not Madame Bovary. What's more, Hortense is beautiful, young, a heroine, and I am not young, not handsome, and not heroic: Père Sinouls and Jim Wedderburn (Laurie's associate) (himself a novelist, but an English novelist, the lucky chap) agree on this point: "You are no hero."

When my novel appeared, I was full of hope. To give you an idea of the full extent of my disappointment, I think it best I place before your eyes some meaningful extracts from my (unpublished) correspondence with my Publisher. I present it to you Such As It Is. I have merely omitted certain proper names to avoid any lawsuits.

One last point of information: my novel is, like all contemporary French novels, a plagiarized version of *Gone with the Wind.*

* * *

Letter from the Author to the Publisher
on the occasion of proofreading the galleys
of his novel entitled Our Beautiful Heroine

Square des Grands-Edredons, 4 March 19..

Dear Publisher,
  You have gladly entrusted me with the proofreading of the galleys of a novel by a certain Jacques Roubaud entitled *Our Beautiful Heroine*. I have carried out this task and I sent them back to you corrected by return mail with the hope that you will kindly forward to me in exchange the galleys for *my* novel entitled *Our Beautiful Heroine*. The novel you have sent me, I must inform you, possesses some *very strong similarities* with my own, so many that it would be vulnerable, if it were to see the light of print, to a charge of plagiarism: indeed, it coincides *word for word* with my own, except for the space separating the 28th character of the 7th line from the bottom of page 168 of my typewritten manuscript and the end of the 18th line at the bottom of page 169, whose words have been replaced by *blank space,* numbered (hypothetically since missing) page 219.
  Inspector Blognard, to whom I at once posed the problem, is categorical: there is *very slight chance* that this is a case of mere coincidence.
  Furthermore, the "plagiarist" (if "plagiarist" there be, something I fear but dare not assert) is assuredly, according to the inspector, Poldevian. Indeed, it can be noted that the majority of the parentheses opened in the text *are not closed* (they are closed elsewhere perhaps, but in that case, *where?*). Now it is known that in logic the so-called *Polish* notation uses only *parentheses that open.* But the Polish notation is, in fact, *Poldevian,* like its inventor, Professor Lukasiewyczmanskoï. CQFD (and QED).

With warmest authorial wishes,
The Author

PS. I have heard (I dare not believe it) that this year you plan to publish books *other than my own.* Are you not afraid of causing a regrettable confusion in the mind of the public, and thus jeopardize the space available in stores for my work, and damage your reputation as well?

Sixth Letter from the Author to the Publisher

The City, 53 Rue des Citoyens, . . . 19..

The Author of the novel *Our Beautiful Heroine,* novel, to the Publisher of the novel *Our Beautiful Heroine,* novel.

Dear Publisher,

In accordance with our agreement, on . . . . . (I withhold the date for reasons of security), the Official Publication Day of My Novel, I went to three City bookstores, chosen at random on the Map using the so-called Monte Carlo method, recommended, as you know, by François Le Lionnais, President-Founder and Freshident-Pounder of OuLiPo, and his Secretary, Marcel Duchamp.

I was expecting to see the shelves cleared of all their extraneous and useless books, the tables loaded with even fourteen-book stacks of my novel, reinforced by a few copies (less numerous and more discreetly displayed) of volumes that might shed light on and further the reading of my own work:

—*Pierrot mon ami* by Raymond Queneau;

—*Einführung in die Theorie der Elektrizität und des Magnetismus* by Max Planck (Heidelberg Edition, 1903);

—the *Prolegomena rhythmorum* by Father Risolnus;

—*The Provençal Cook* by Reboul;

—*Adversos mathematicos* by Sextus Empiricus.

I pictured with great pleasure the lines of potential customers for my book, guided by comely salesgirls, furnished with a customer service number and a personal information sheet stating their age, sax (I've put down the word *sax* to avoid any legal action), their first name and their profession, heading toward the table where a copy, especially conceived with them in mind, furnished with a computer-generated dedication, would be handed over to them, in exchange for their money.

What was my surprise to observe that, not only had the necessary measures not been taken, but these three bookstores *continued to sell books other than my own* (including, I say this painfully and without recriminations, but I cannot not say it, *books published by you yourself*, my dear Publisher [did you not read the postscriptum to my first letter?]). My mind becomes muddled speculating on the reasons for this inopportune turn of events: chance? misunderstanding? *sabotage!!!* I have not yet been able to widen my investigation to other bookstores because of a regrettable wrist-sprain that occurred while I was clearing, with all due energy, the third of these stores' tables of those untimely books that were hampering my own. Moreover, Père Sinouls, whom I immediately called upon, is unfortunately confined to his bed of pain as a result, and I quote, "of the sciatica he caught while listening, snug in his blankets, to the morning radio broadcast of an exercise program." In addition, it set off his tennis elbow again. I am at a loss as to what to do.

With great sorrow, but
always,
your, comma,

Author

P.S. I bring to your attention, perhaps you have not been so informed, that an important article has just appeared in the *Indépendent des Côtes Sud du Minervois-Nord.* Here is the text:

"Jackes Roubod: *Our Lovely Heroine.* Absolutely read this if you have nothing else to do and no more bedtime herbal tea within reach."

Preserving, thanks to the photocopy, only the first three words of the article, it could serve to our advantage in ads, don't you agree?

Letter 6-A from the Author to the Publisher
(the same day)

Immediately following the word "your" at the end of my preceding letter, instead of:

", comma,"

read:

quote unquote, ","

Sincerely

The Author

P.S. The words "quote unquote," comma, above, are useless. Period. But since I am out of correcting tape and Père Sinouls is unavailable to replace it, because of his gout complicated by tennis elbow, I have not unfortunately been able to erazzze them.

(Correspondence continued in chapter 18)

Chapter 10

Inspector Sheralockiszyku Holamesidjudjy

We left Inspector Blognard in the Church of Sainte-Gudule before the dead body of Balbastre, Père Sinouls's murdered dog. His gaze, sharp as a laser, which had been directed toward Madame Eusèbe, had been momentarily interrupted and we rejoin it now. For us, in the interval, many things have happened, but for his part, the inspector had just taken leave of Père Sinouls. Père Sinouls and he are old acquaintances; they met at the time of the horrible Case, dubbed The Hardware Store Horror, and afterward during its no less atrocious sequel called The Case of the Dry Cleaner Wrangler. When he has the time, the inspector comes over for discussions with Père Sinouls; he brings along Arapède who engages Sinouls in a few skeptic arguments. Père Sinouls and Madame Blognard try to outdo each other with their stews and *coqs au vin*. But today is, alas, no time for cooking and conversation.

Père Sinouls is a friend, but is he not, however unlikely, however frightening it may seem, a suspect? Does his unaffected pain spring from sorrow, or remorse? Masters have been known to murder their dogs (more often the opposite). Blognard has no choice but to ponder all these things, which is not much to his liking. He shakes Père Sinouls's hand and turns toward Madame Eusèbe. But he does not have the leisure to follow his intuition, for once again he must do something else. This time he is called to the phone. We use this opportunity to return to the scene; we have lost almost nothing of narrative substance.

64

Who was calling Blognard? Once again it was Joubert, the Big Boss. There were no two ways about it (nor six ways, as at Bobigny for example (get off at the second most beautiful City station: Bobigny-Pantin-Raymond Queneau (the most beautiful is P . . .))).

"Blognard, this case is of the utmost delicacy!" Blognard heard on the phone, "I know dog murders generally fall outside your line but I am taking advantage of the fact that Booled'Hogg (the inspector heading the Canine Brigade) is working full time on the Ventoux Case (a gang of very senior citizens, quite radical leftwingers, were burglarizing supermarkets to steal supplies of Ventoux, Cuisine for Dogs with Class; they distributed them afterward free of charge to elderly people in the City) to put you on the case. Monsignor Fustiger has just called me again; the Ministry of the Interior and the Archdiocese agree to place someone at your disposal to help you. I cannot refuse. He's a Poldevian inspector, a super-superintendent, their shrewdest sleuth, so I'm told. His name is, his name is . . . the paper, for God's sake, not my wife's laundry bill, what a ninny! I don't mean you, Blognard, I'm talking to my secretary . . . good, it's about time, his name is Sheralockiszyku Holamesidjudjy, or something close; fine then, I must be going, good luck!"

And at that precise moment, the Poldevian inspector led by Arapède, appeared before Blognard:

"My name is Shurelykasiko Halimysudjedjo," he said.

"Hello   Inspector Blognard   I presume?   I believe? I am certain?

"Honored   I honorablissimly am extremelissimly extremely

"The most famousissimos   and Blognard inspectors inspectorissimos   of working   with   Arapède

"Modelissimos   you are Poldevia like models in my country   beenings

65

"of deduction   deductive of the honorabile art de-
tectivissmo   artistic
"of copperating with you   weakissimo but full of good
will and humblissimly   with all my powers   and I will
strive

"I am certain?   Hello I believe?   Inspector I presume?
Blognard
"extremely   honored   extremilissimly   I am honor-
abillissimly
"Arapède   the famousissimo   with   and Blognard   of
working inspectorissimos inspectors
"beenings   modelissimos   in my country   you are   like
models   Poldevia
"artistic   of deduction   detectivissimos   deductive
honorabilish   of the art
"and I will strive   to copperate with you   with all my
powers   weakissimo   and humblissimo   but full of good
will

"Blognard   I am certain?   I presume?   Hello   Inspector
I believe?
"Honorabilissimily   extremely   am   honored
extremelissimly
"inspectors inspectorissimos   Arapède   of working
the famousissimo   and Blognard with
"Poldevia   beenings   like models   modelissimos   you
are   in my country
"of the artistic art   honorable   of deduction   deductive
detectivissimo
"but full of good will   and I will strive   in my humblish
of copperating with you   weakissimo   with all my power

....
....

66

....

....

....

....

......

......

"I am certain   Honored   Blognard   Model   Detectivissimo   In my humblish   Will   "
(the fading lines of dots mark the fading attention of Blognard
during the Poldevian inspector's introductory remarks)
There was a silence of sorts.

            *   *   *

Blognard turned toward Arapède.
"What's he saying?"
"He's speaking our language," Arapède said delicately.
"Ah," said Blognard, not much more enlightened for all of
that. "Translate."
Stripped of all subtleties resulting from the permutation
of repetitions, as well as the most essential threats and
nuances, reduced to the crudest superficiality, said Arapède,
who knew Poldevian, the message goes as follows: after
uttering his name the inspector indicated he was in the act
of supposing that he was addressing you. He added that he
was happy to be working with us because in his country our
reputation is rather good (slightly above average if I correctly
understood the positions of the adverbs) and that he would
try to help us to the extent our investigation does not
damage the vital interests of Poldevia.
"Ah," said Blognard. "They talk that way all the time, do
they?"

67

"No," said Arapède, "it's the translation in our language devised by the inspector to take into account the well-recognized slowness of understanding on the part of foreigners (regarding Poldevia, of course) and of the poor thought-content of their linguistic expressions."

"Ah," said Blognard, who felt an irresistible propensity to monosyllabism (which is not necessarily associated, as is often believed, with monotheism). "This is going to take a while."

It did. Inspector She. Hol. (from now on we will call him She. Hol. for reasons of brevity; which is to say that henceforth, and for the remainder of the novel, excepting express mention of the contrary, the expression She. Hol. composed by the typographic signs S,h,e,. H,o,l., the sign H being preceded by a blank, will designate the Poldevian inspector), Inspector She. Hol. informed Blognard and Arapède of the following facts (as a result of an out-and-out power play on the part of the Publisher, the forty-seven pages of dialogue between the inspectors, containing all the necessary nuances, have been removed from the galleys and replaced by the following summary, for which the Author declines all responsibility):

There're these six princes in Poldevia; there's this Prince Regent, Gormanskoï, who is rather a nice fellow, as far as this affair goes at any rate, and there're these five other princes, which makes six (five plus one makes six); one of these other princes, who is not reigning, would like to be Prince Regent; he deems he has the right. His name is *K'manoroïgs*. Prince Gormanskoï, for personal and amorous reasons, has been absent from Poldevia for several months. Prince K'manoroïgs would be pleased if he were never to come back and resume his place. It so happens that the princes look a lot alike; they are all practically indistinguishable Handsome Young Men; they all have a great gift for disguise. How can they be told apart? One way alone: their trademark, located on the left buttock. It's a snail spiral (the snail is the sacred animal of the Poldevians); each has the same but with a subtle difference. Six groups of dots are tattooed inside the spiral; they are numbered, but differently for each prince.

K'manoroïgs's plan is simple. Having murdered Balbastre (he is certainly the culprit), get Gormanskoï arrested in his place, and calmly return to Poldevia to be Prince Regent. One last detail: the religion of each prince is different. Prince K'manoroïgs's is Computeric. He's a top-notch programmer.

Chapter 11

Reflections on Marriage

And by the morning of the murder, things still hadn't been set right, quite to the contrary.

This last phrase of the encroachment on our chapter 4 is intended to facilitate our return to Hortense, after a long journey that led us:

—from the Gudule Bar to Laurie and Carlotta's apartment while following the Author;

—from 53 Rue des Citoyens, D stairway, to the Poldevian Chapel's hidden lean-to (flashback);

—from the lean-to to Sainte-Gudule to meet Inspector She. Hol.

And here we are once more back in the Gudule Bar, owned by Madame Yvonne, who has a new waiter, a Handsome Young Man. We resolutely respect a topological concentration upon the area specified on the map sold with this volume (see page 135).

We are in the Gudule Bar and Laurie is on her second coffee, lighting a blue Jack-Please cigarette. Hortense bites into her slice of bread generously buttered by Madame Yvonne who thinks she's a bit skinny-sickly pale these days. She wipes her lips with her paper napkin; she's a very well-mannered young lady.

"You were right," she said, "he's jealous. There's no other explanation. What am I going to do?"

"There's a cure for jealousy," Laurie answered. "But I don't have the time to talk; plus I'm still not awake."

Père Sinouls's phone call threw her to the foot of her bed

and she had begun her day in the reverse of her natural order: she had gone out before being awake, before having her tea and her shower, and she had already had coffee without having tea. Everything was profoundly disrupted. She glanced out the window, spotted the clock of Sainte-Gudule and recoiled in horror at the time: "It's not possible; its not after noon! I'm already late!" She had to meet her associate, Jim Wedderburn, in the square, and he rose early and was punctual. Fortunately he was still on English time and for him it was still only nine in the morning.

"See you later," Laurie said, "I'll call you tonight."

And she left.

They had met in a shop: Laurie was buying a scanty Day-Glo tangerine undergarment (how far away it all is, she thought, remembering the first time they exchanged smiles) and Hortense was buying the same thing but in Day-Glo sky-blue. They smiled at each other, then went out, then in the same direction, then had coffee, then saw each other again, then found they had a great deal in common on different subjects; and Laurie mentioned several movies to Hortense, who lent her several books and vice versa. Hortense took Laurie to hear Agamben, who spoke to them of Plato's seventh letter with such conviction and subtlety that they thought they understood for a moment, which made them pretty happy; then they again spoke of things closer at hand and drank Guinness at Laurie's second headquarters (there was the Nearby Headquarters for morning coffee, which was the Gudule Bar, and there was General Headquarters, for the late afternoon Guinness, which was a little farther toward the center of town, at the Imperial Sentier qui Bifurque). Then Hortense invited Laurie to dinner but that didn't sit too well with her husband. And Hortense came for dinner over at D stairway. Armance was there with her boyfriend Pib who worked twenty-six hours a day at revolutionizing

71

sixth generation computer role-playing; and they drank *blanc cassis,* they ate squid with cucumbers and spices, and *fromage blanc.* Hortense was delighted. But not with her life, which did not strike her as going quite as it should by comparison. The mirror of her life reflected an image of herself that was not much to her liking.

*   *   *

Speaking of image, Hortense, once Laurie left, remained lost in thought in the middle of her slice of bread. This image should not be taken literally: I mean that Hortense is not between two pieces of bread spelled out in letters, but only that she has suspended her butter-bread swallowing activity while Laurie was leaving the Gudule Bar and that her slice is not yet all eaten.

She really could not say why, but she found herself remembering with a tender nostalgia the blessed times when she woke up alone in her large apartment which still belonged all to her and to her alone. It was after her lover Morgan left (whose real name, Prince Gormanskoï, you have the right to know). It was before Morgan deceived and betrayed her, no doubt; it's true, he had deceived and betrayed her; he was a burglar: not through moral abasement nor harsh economic necessity but through a simple atavistic calling genetically and culturally determined by his origins, those of a distant land, whose criteria are so different from our own, whose history, geography, verily verily this side of the Pyrenees, wrong, the other side, unless maybe it's the Alps,

(we are, as you suspect, presently in the thick of a rather special novelistic sequence, technically termed an "interior monologue." Both you, my faithful Reader, and I have penetrated in small-scale model form naturally, immaterially and impalpably, through Hortense's left ear, which has a small particularly succulent lobe for lovers' incisors, and we are navigating through her cerebral circumvolutions [rather charming, as is the rest of Hortense's person; not only are Hortense's exterior surfaces and "volumes" likely to fall under the snipping scissors of the censors Mister Q-isn't-that-so and Reckless Disregard, but also her brain and her thoughts]. We collect the fragments of thought animating her while she is musing, between two half-slices, elbows on the café table, in the already waning coolness of this warm spring morning. We collect her thoughts and we translate them into a "modified interior monologue," that is, without seeking to reproduce the discontinuities, imprecisions and digressions of every sort which occur in Hortense's day-dream. End of the technical parentheses]

Morgan, she thought, was a burglar unlike any other and had been a marvelous lover (a gentle reminiscent warmth suffused her), it's true he should not have burglarized *her too*, without any risk even at that, taking advantage of her full and absolute trust, of her unforgivable naïveté, of her naïve knees as well, and he especially shouldn't have, he shouldn't have stolen her shoes she could not not continue thinking that she'd been right not to forgive him and to dis-inlove him when she had discovered the truth and at any rate, it was too late she would never see him again never what a horrible word, *never,* she had fallen into marriage how else to say it but fallen and was this what marriage was all about? that's why the real life experience was kept hushed up she had let herself get caught in this business and what a pain a jealous husband is and especially over nothing at all what am I going to do with my life now my life's a rotten mess, thought Hortense, and her eyes welled with tears (notice how interior monologue tends to eliminate punctuation) she had to do something to talk to someone there was only Laurie but Laurie couldn't in the morning generally and there was no point in waiting for something from Laurie before five in the evening she just had to understand that

and why bother her friend with that you don't go around
bothering your friends with every little problem like life love
and marriage but on the other hand she had to talk she was
not able to continue on like this in silence fatality and regret
life messed up by overharshness it's true he shouldn't have
swiped her shoes and her dresses her dresses too and her
jewels it's true he had swiped her dresses to sell Oh Morgan
you shouldn't have Oh Morgan you abandoned and betrayed
me and look what's happened now I'm the wife of a jealous
man!... Her thoughts began to turn in circles and we as
well, navigator-explorers of the charming fog of Hortense's
brain, we are beginning to get dizzy with these thoughts
turning in circles although I ask you my friend my Reader
does the fact that Hortense's thoughts are turning in circles
necessarily mean that their mnestic brain-route is necessarily circular perhaps it's elliptical helicoidal perhaps
perhaps there's even a rather warped homeomorphism
between thought and brain of the inside-out variety I don't
know   my apologies I'm the one who's starting to monologue interiorwise now and if I'm in Hortense's so charming
brain interior there is no reason for you to be forced to look
into mine which has no charm whatsoever...

The tears now ran openly from Hortense's beautiful gray
eyes, they ran into her slice of bread and her cold milk.

"Come, come now, Hortense," said Madame Yvonne, "you
mustn't cry over nothing, you'll see the man you love again."

Hortense blew her nose into her Kleenex, wiped her beautiful gray eyes clouded with tears, thanked Madame Yvonne
and left. She knew what she had to do: speak to Père Sinouls.

Chapter 12

Preparation for an Introduction
to Beeranalysis

Hortense left the Gudule Bar still wiping away her tears that kept flowing like nostalgia. The sunlight stung her eyes. She headed toward the square, her steps tentative but more determined as she walked along, even though she had decided to go see Père Sinouls. A glance at the Area Map (page 135) shows us that we have a contradiction of sorts here: to get to Père Sinouls's place you must take Rue des Milleguiettes; therefore, if coming out of the Gudule Bar, you must turn *right* on Rue des Grands-Edredons. And that's not what Hortense was doing!

And if that had been what Hortense did, we would have taken a detour toward a completely different novel than the one you are in the midst of living while reading. At every moment, it is true, in novels as in life, forking paths appear and choices, alas, must be made. At times you experience a momentary hesitation of sorts, you go off on a digression, but it's a rather dangerous affair. You are fully aware of this upon entering it, but you don't know when you'll come back out. You might very well forget to return: the unpenetrated forest of other possible adventures looms before us, offering its mysteries. You disappear into it a few steps and suddenly hesitate: another path arises, with another fork. Why not open a second digression, a digression within a digression, and so on? And you never get back on the way.

I would have liked very much to explore certain of these parallel fictional universes, and I had proposed to my

Publisher, in spite of the enormous amount of additional work it would have imposed upon me, to furnish him with an absolute forest of multiple diverging and reconverging tales, with approved spatio-temporal travel maps, and a guide provided for the tourists of the fiction. The same unchangeable book would not have been stupidly printed for everyone but, rediscovering good old thirteenth-century customs (it was only yesterday), during the age of manuscripts, each reader would have his *own personalized book*. The book would not be available in stores. Or rather, in good bookstores, you would have had the chance to choose: either the standard edition, everybody's book (excellent, certainly, as are all the Author's books, the bookstore clerk would have said), or else you would have placed an order for *your* edition, chosen according to a "menu" of possible forkings in the course of the tale. This copy *would not yet have been printed*. By pressing here and there on a keyboard, the bookstore clerk would have transmitted to the computer-printer the specifications of the novel chosen by the customer and at once, thanks to modern typesetting/composition processes, vroom, vroom, the book would be on its way; and it would arrive in no time. Père Sinouls assures me that this is within the realm of possibility *at the present moment,* but that the large publishing houses are against it, for they want to clear out their soon unsellable stocks of compact discs. (I don't grasp the connection very well, but Père Sinouls is quite positive: he has it from the female cousin of a salesman in a big shopping mall; plus it confirms what he always thought.)

You see the beauty of the thing: the Reader would have received a unique copy, unlike any other; and he would have, by his choices, participated in the act of creation. Creativity is the Future (with participation). The book he would have read would have been read by *no one else,* not even by the Author.

Thus for books, each one distinct, there would have been

equally distinct readers. I suppose that all readers are distinct (if you buy two copies of the same book at different moments, they will still be different, the moment of the request being subtly incorporated in the choices carried out by the computer-printer, and to my mind this means there is Another Reader), but at the same time the readers would not have been totally separated from each other, for the stories told in different versions would have had many points in common (everything would have been written by me); they would have intersected, intertangled, confirmed (or contradicted) each other without ever disappearing into the infinite distance of private, implacably foreign worlds. Naturally my work would have been increased tenfold, a hundredfold, but what does that matter? I was ready to dedicate myself accordingly and thus advance the art of the novel. Well, you're not going to believe me, but as incredible as it may seem, my Publisher did not want to hear about it for more than thirty-seven seconds. Therefore you will never know what would have happened if, instead of leaving for the square, Hortense had gone directly to Père Sinouls's place (upon reflection, I realize that even if you were to have known what was going to happen in this hypothesis, you would not then have known what you are about to know now, what Hortense is going to do in this novel, the only one to have finally been written; it's disturbing, but I don't have the time to linger upon this question).

*   *   *

Crossing the square, Hortense spotted Laurie wrapped up in conversation with her associate Jim Wedderburn; she saw Jim Wedderburn, and we saw him too, since we were in the process of following Hortense. Please note this fact. She gave them a little wave without stopping, turned onto Rue de l'Abbé-Migne while passing as far away as possible from the

Eusèbe grocery and Eusèbe the grocer's gnosistological eyes, turned left on Rue des Citoyens and went into the Groichant Bakery, located on the opposite sidewalk, in front of the rear exit to Sainte-Gudule, called the worshipers' exit because of the almost direct access it offered to Monsieur Groichant's justly renowned cream puffs.

And why? Because she hadn't finished her slice of bread, which would no longer have been simply buttered, but buttered and salted because of the tears she had shed on top. She was still hungry. Madame Groichant was seated, majestic and creamy, behind her counter. She was in the full bloom of her beauty, half "nun" (I'm referring to the double-decker chocolate éclair, not the vocation), half vacherin (I'm referring to the pastry, not the cheese), in her full bloom of beauty between two little Groichants (the tenth and eleventh, I believe). She greeted Hortense affectionately and anxiously; she found her paler, listless. Marriage had not done wonders for her, quite the opposite. Madame Groichant was not surprised, what with that husband of hers who was never around to look after her. Hortense had been employed for a time in the Groichant Bakery and was under the culinary protection of Madame Groichant, who prepared small packages of cakes for her to stimulate her appetite. There were few people in the store; only Madame Groichant's new pastry boy, humming a popular song while carrying in the last cream puffs:

> Linzer torte
> In the Dead Sea
> Takes on a caramel tint
> But in Alsace
> It's potash
> That gives its honey hue.

(Music by Wolfgang Amadeus Mozart, K.331, first movement, rondo; words by the Author.)

Hortense glanced at him while kissing Madame Groichant. He was a Handsome Young Man, if not an extremely Handsome Young Man. She thought that there were suddenly quite a lot of Handsome Young Men (without counting the pretty boys) in the neighborhood. After her marriage it had seemed to her that all the Handsome Young Men had more or less disappeared and here they were abruptly reappearing. They could even be seen on television. The last time she went to Laurie's, Carlotta had shown her part of a commercial that she had recorded on her VCR before a Dew-Pon Dew-Val concert. She saw again (and we see in Hortense's eyes, please note) the Handsome Young Man draw close, on the beach, to the water's edge. Reaching it, he slowly took off his jeans and stood in minuscule bathing shorts in all his glory. The female bathers, stretched on the sand of the commercial at the edge of the blue sea of the commercial, leaned up on an elbow to look at him, as Hortense herself had done. He slowly turned around, but they didn't see the end of the commercial with the brand name of the jeans, no doubt because Carlotta had cut the scene so as not to miss one bit of Dew-Pon Dew-Val. Hortense remembered this image and it threw her into turmoil. She felt cold, she felt hot, her middle regions quivered as they hadn't for ages. And once more she thought: oh Morgan oh Morgan why have you abandoned me?

Père Sinouls was in his garden, surrounded by telegrams of condolence. He cast Hortense a questioning glance.

"I've come for a session," she said.

Part Three

Passion

Chapter 13

Introduction to Beeranalysis

While typing "Chapter 13" above I felt a reluctance of sorts on the part of my typewriter. There is a problem with thirteenth chapters. After thirteenth floors in hotels disappeared, Americans eliminated page thirteens in newspapers and more recently chapter 13s in all novels (including the new editions of novels written when people still wrote chapter 13s). Putting a chapter 13 into a novel appears, nowadays, like an outmoded antiquarian Old World novelist's custom. I decided however to maintain it for the following reason: in my book, numbers play an important role, especially in their even and odd distinction. It is not immaterial for a character, or for his reactions, to figure in an even or in an odd chapter. If I eliminate chapter 13, chapter 14 comes immediately after chapter 12. That turns chapter 14 into an *uneven* chapter, since chapter 12, its predecessor, is, you will agree, an *even* chapter. But the *number fourteen* does not become, for all of that, an odd number; it remains even as usual. There exists a discrepancy here, a glaring kin to the one pointed out by President Le Lionnais in his *Dictionary of Noteworthy Numbers:* is 13-A even, or odd? Eliminating chapter 13 would therefore introduce a numerical doubt concerning evenness which would inevitably and negatively influence the characters subjected to this uncertainty. I cannot pull such a stunt on Père Sinouls who plays the central role in this chapter, seeing how he has just lost his dog Balbastre, murdered in such a cowardly way.

But (Reader, you say to me), what about the American

translation? This is a real problem: since I plan on an American translation of my book (different from the English translation where such questions do not yet arise), ought I not to take measures, since chapter 13 will be eliminated at any rate, so that it not contain any essential development, that it be a transitional chapter that can be cut without harming the rest of the story? But here once again, I am helpless. I cannot eliminate from this chapter what comprises its particular attraction: a survey of Beeranalysis, invented by Père Sinouls, which I was not able to take up in chapter 12, as a result of Hortense being delayed along her way.

I therefore had to retain a chapter 13. So here we go.

What is Beeranalysis? Let us examine the composition and etymology of the word. *Beer* comes from English and means "beer," which in turn comes from the German word *bier* (in French *bière*). *Analysis* contains *ana,* as in "Anna." Finally there is *lysis,* which serves to end the word harmoniously. Beer + Anna + Lysis gives us "Beeranalysis."

Beeranalysis follows a number of other x-analyses, of which it is the crowning achievement: first there was Alfred Jarry's Patanalysis; there was Psychoanalysis with its various old or recent branches like Simpanalysis by Julio Bouddheveau. And Père Sinouls, finally, invented Beeranalysis.

Here's how it works: the male, or female, patient enters Père Sinouls's office. There is a desk, an armchair in front of the desk, a lamp and papers on the desk. There is a couch. So far, nothing really new. But careful now: in the majority of classic analyses the patient stretches out on the couch and talks. The analyst is seated at his desk and reads his mail. Père Sinouls had put into effect an epistemological break of crucial importance, which would be henceforth inescapable.

He is the one who stretches out on the couch with his beer. The male/female analysand sits at the desk and talks.

Why beer? To evoke a publike atmosphere (which explains

the English word *beer*) conducive to speech; let us examine, for example, a typical English family at mealtime. The father is reading his *Times*, behind which he entirely disappears. The mother is nervously bustling back and forth from the dining room to the kitchen to check on her "casserole" (French recipe). The children are neither seen nor heard. Silence. In order to speak, they go to the pub. That is what gave Père Sinouls the idea for beer.

After a while, he would fall asleep and start snoring. That was an essential point of the method: for if the patient stopped talking, he would wake up Père Sinouls with his abrupt silence, and the session would be a failure. Therefore he had to talk, keep talking, he was forced to talk, struck by the thought of the possible, then probable, then imminent moment Père Sinouls would wake up. Here again the pub comparison is inescapable: consider the feverishness that sweeps pubs when serving hours are drawing to an end, when the closing-time bell rings out. Père Sinouls maintained something similar: for if the patient continued talking (thus a successful session), he interrupted the session by an automatic and infallible procedure. The more the words flowed, the deeper he sank into his sleep. Then his hand dropped the glass of beer, his wrist turned and his *Poldevian wrist-alarm* said *I love you* (in Poldevian). Père Sinouls would wake up and the session was over.

Let us mention, out of thoroughness, another *crucial reversal* of classic analyses: Beeranalysis was *entirely free of charge*. What's more, if it was the right time, Père Sinouls provided lunch.

*   *   *

Hortense sat at the desk and talked. But she didn't stay for lunch because she had to get home and fix her husband's. Père Sinouls suggested a menu in accordance with what he

85

had just heard during the session. He was asleep during the sessions, of course, but he heard very well what was said to him; it passed directly into his dreams, thus nurturing, unawares, the staggering aptness of his diagnoses and advice.

Once again alone, Père Sinouls decided to go to work.

Since Père Sinouls was the organist at Sainte-Gudule's, we think we are going to attend free of charge one of his concerts, whose program we can already imagine: a bit of Bach, a bit of Pachelbel, maybe some Buxtehude, and then wrapping up with a nice big choral piece by Praetorius, for example. A serious mistake. Père Sinouls was in the thick of a mid-life fling: he was stricken by a passion for computers.

This is how it came upon him: during his gout attacks (more and more frequent), touching the organ keyboard was virtually impossible; it drew cries of pain from him. But, more generally and ontologically, with the onset of age, he had grown tired of playing his instrument like a deaf man for the deaf. He wanted to play only when he felt like it (and sometimes he would feel like it), but most of all he had had enough of his organ. He wanted to try new ones, go out on a few concert tours: organs, wines and cheeses of the Loire; organs and pubs of Kent, for example. There were so many things that interested him more than his work: reading the very latest science fiction, discussing "our beautiful society" with old buddies, the Author among them, perfecting his Beeranalysis by listening to a beautiful young woman full of exciting problems, arguing with his daughters, yelling at his wife, his son, etc.

He then got the inspired, brilliant idea: he was slicing some potatoes Julie had skinned for a gratin Dauphinois in order to make a comparison with Laurie's when the knife suddenly slipped and his finger was magnificently opened; it gushed blood everywhere. Julie took him to the hospital but, the whole while, he thought about his sublime, illuminating idea: if he himself doesn't want to play his organ, then "x" must play in his place. But "x" can be no mercenary individual, for:

—if he pays "x," no more money for beer, science fiction, compact discs, not to mention the steak for feeding those dear heads (red and blond in particular);

—if he doesn't pay "x," what "x" is going to want to play in his place?

It follows that "x" could not be a member of the human race. Therefore let's consider a tape recording. OK. Let's say there's a tape recorded by "y." But "y" cannot be an individual belonging to the human race, if "y" is indeed a variant of "x." In fact Chapuis or Isoir might be given consideration, by putting to use one of their very pricey compact discs. But just listening to Mazalor, especially if a person has a good ear, would be detected right away and Sinouls ran the risk of being fired on the spot. Of necessity therefore it was imperative that:

$x = y = $ Sinouls.

We have not made much progress, you think, for we have apparently returned to the point we started at: if, in order not to have to play the organ, Sinouls must record himself playing, what has been gained?

Here is where the ingeniousness of the Sinoulsian idea shines forth. He will make a computer do the playing. The computer would learn to play in the inimitable Sinoulsian style, it would produce pure Sinouls, and meanwhile Sinouls himself would have a rest.

The problem, then, was subdivided into two parts:

—a mechanism had first to be perfected which, while he calmly installed himself in front of his keyboard with his SF, would relay the program to the computer. This was the easiest part, such thingamajigs already being available on the market. In fact (but here money was a special problem which could be solved only by resolving the second half of the problem), he could do much better: install a robot that would play (i.e., activate the computer) in his place and he would not even need to show up anymore (thanks to a remote control) in person in front of his keyboard;

—there remained the music. He needed:

a) a computer;

b) to learn how to use it so as to develop the musical software able to realize his deliverance.

Thanks to his friends at the Center of Comparative Pataphysics, based very nearby on Rue Vieille-des-Archives in the Hotel of the Poldevian Ambassadors (an old seventeenth-century hotel), he easily secured the loan of a computer with the required flexibility. He first set it up quite openly in his bedroom. But after displaying great patience, Madame Sinouls finally said: "It's her or me. Either your mistress leaves our marital home, or I'm going back to mother's."

And that's why, in order to go to work, Père Sinouls was obliged to traverse the forty-nine yards separating him from the small room where his computer rested.

Chapter 14

Birth of a Multinational

There are three benches in Square des Grands-Edredons on the Sainte-Gudule side. Each bench is overshadowed by a tree: a chestnut tree toward Rue des Grands-Edredons, a linden in the middle, and a Judas tree on the Poldevian Chapel side. Noon was drawing near; the screeching hordes of children had disappeared into the neighboring houses to tank up (with hamburgers and other stuff) before reattacking sand and ears. The only one left behind was a little four-year-old boy filling his bucket with soil, which he would then moisten at the fountain, only to return and deposit his mud-brew cake in homage at the feet of Laurie, who was sitting on the middle bench amid the scent of the linden.

The sun was rising, with some hesitation, as if this sudden drop in decibels disconcerted him. He did not dare to move too far along his orbit, so as not to disturb Laurie, who had her eyes closed and seemed happy and at peace with her lot, bathed in light and heat.

This bench, the central bench of the square, therefore of the neighborhood, was the one where, in the past, Inspector Blognard, disguised as a bum, wearing a beret sprinkled with frying oil, a bathrobe of old Pyrenean wool, and sewer worker's boots, had spent countless hours tracking the daring criminal who was called The Hardware Store Horror. Looking up, all the windows of 53 Rue des Citoyens were in view, as well as those on Rue des Grands-Edredons, at least as far as the Gudule Bar. The clouds, when they arrived on the square, coming out from behind the shoulder of Sainte-

Gudule's, lingered as if suspended, displaying a certain reluctance to continue on their way, so much did they envy the calm and serenity of the spot; but the wind pushed them on and they left in spite of themselves to rain on the province of Lorraine, while cursing their nomad existence. At this moment, the sky was a pure, airy blue. Through her eyelids, where rested a gentle layer of spring sunshine, Laurie could make out, vaguely, through the panes of the large room the dangerous forward and backward leaps of her daughter Carlotta, who thus joyously dissipated a small part of the boundless animal spirits filling her to exuberance.

There was a little bit of noise: the older brother of the little boy with the red bucket and mud-brew had come to get the child. While leaving, he shouted to Laurie: "Mademoiselle, Mademoiselle, say I'll be your fiancé, I'm free."

The square was empty.

Entering the Gudule Bar, Laurie spotted on TV the young man who was walking on the beach. He drew close to the edge of the sea, very maritime with its blue waves, took off his jeans, and stood with nothing on but his skimpy bathing suit. As on the other occasions, the female bathers lying on the sand leaned up to look at him because he was a Handsome Young Man. He did not give them so much as a glance, but turned toward the still distant silhouette of a dog who was running toward him across the sand. The young man held his jeans in his hand and as the camera closed in to show the brand, it seemed to Laurie that he had a tattoo on one buttock: it appeared vaguely at the very edge of his bathing suit, but the image was suddenly interrupted, for Madame Yvonne had changed the channel.

The waiter smiled at her. She ordered a cup of coffee with a glass of water.

What made Laurie pensive was not so much her lack of

sleep and the pleasant drowsiness caused by the sunshine in the square, but her conversation with her associate, Jim Wedderburn. As we have already repeated several times, Laurie had an associate, whose name was Jim Wedderburn. The word *associate* seems to indicate a business venture. We are not mistaken. It is indeed a business venture, and what's more one in the process of great expansion, which was the joint property of Laurie and Jim Wedderburn. And their business expansion was such that it was beginning to cause problems which preoccupied Laurie. It is therefore necessary to describe it in a few words.

* * *

Jim Wedderburn was English on his mother's side (whose name he had adopted) and Poldevian on his father's, whom he declared he never knew. He lived in London in the basement of a mews lost deep in the Royal Borough of Kensington and Chelsea. There he wrote novels, spending, for food, the limited Poldevian funds willed him by his father, which allowed him a modest but comfortable life. He wrote, I said, novels: English novels. I do indeed mean English novels, not English-language novels. (How can the English novel be recognized? By a certain whiff of Englishness that is unmistakable.) His first novel was entitled *Finite Corpse*. He had written five, fallen into pleasant obscurity following publication, when the sixth, to his great surprise as well as his publisher's, took off on the best-seller list. It must be acknowledged that this novel differed somewhat from the five others, perhaps less an English novel than they. The title was *Lady Bovary's Lover*.

Jim Wedderburn watched with interest the arrival of a likely financial ease which would allow him to continue writing obscurely pleasant English novels for several years without having to worry about tomorrow. And most especially he was able to envisage fulfilling his lifelong dream: traveling through the vast world and visiting every bookstore. Bookstores were his only, his all-consuming passion. But it was at this moment that catastrophe struck. There lived in Texas a lady by the name of Bovary, you see, who was the widow of a modest oilman who had left her enough to live modestly—a little too modestly for her taste. *Lady Bovary's Lover* had hardly left the U.S. best-seller list (on which it had remained for thirty-seven weeks) when Jim Wedderburn's publisher received in his offices a visit by Messrs. Smallbone and Pettigrew, Boston lawyers. They came over by Concord. They informed him that they were asking, in the name of their client Mrs. Bovary of Paris, Texas, the sum of $1,178,000.00 for "invasion of privacy."

Jim Wedderburn's publisher smiled politely.

"Mr. Wedderburn's novel, gentlemen," he said to them with exquisite politeness, "is in a way a portmanteau novel that could be signed D. H. Flowbert. Lady Bovary does not have, with any really past or present Bovary, and perhaps even future one, anything in common."

"This we know very well," answered Messrs. Smallbone and Pettigrew who were Harvard graduates. "We don't think you get the point."

Certainly, Mrs. Bovary of Paris, Texas, readily recognized (off the record) that Lady Bovary (of the novel) did not resemble her in the least. But that's precisely the reason for her lawsuit: the two Bovarys were so different that it could only seriously damage their client who found herself in the unenviable insomnia-generating position of having to explain to her friends and acquaintances in the Widows' Club of Paris, Texas, that she was not *the spitting image* of the heroine of a book recommended by the *Cowboy Examiner* and which had remained thirty-seven weeks on the best-seller list.

The publisher, at that point, became icy and British. He refused to compromise, went to trial before the Massachusetts District Court and lost.

American law, and jurisprudence, indeed, are clear: all fiction is biographical, such is the first axiom. And, as a second axiom, all biography is an "invasion of privacy." As Judge Nickson explained in his decision: a fiction not in accordance with the visible or hidden biographical data of the plaintiff is a particularly serious slur on her private life since, depicting her as she is not, it spreads doubt about the uprightness, transparence and rectitude of her life among those close to her. The author's obvious good faith is an aggravating circumstance: Not knowing the real life of one's characters is no excuse. He should have made inquiries.

The Publisher immediately turned against Jim Wedderburn, who was again ruined.

He had, most urgently, to earn his living. But how? He was spending his last pounds sterling with a melancholy air in Parisian bookstores when he met Laurie.

They had just bought the same book, a book of Jean-Yves Cousseau photographs. Laurie put her purchase in a plastic bag that she had brought back from the Isle of Ré, Jim put his in a plastic bag that he had been given in a bookstore on the Isle of Man where there are cats of a particular species that is found nowhere else on earth and where Manx is spoken. And Jim Wedderburn thought: "Ah, if only I had a plastic bookstore bag from the Isle of Ré on the soil of which in mid-August Portuguese immigrant workers sing such beautiful *fados.*" That got things off and running: they exchanged bags, they went to Laurie's to celebrate this exchange with a good bottle of Saint-Joseph's white wine and oysters. Thus their small enterprise was born: they would go through the vast world, visit all the bookstores, carrying off plastic bags that they would resell at fabulous prices, or deliver on order. In this way:

—they earned enough to live on;

—they traveled;

—they spent a lot of time in bookstores.

Jim Wedderburn had conquered his destiny.

But Laurie thought that success began to surpass her expectations. Orders flowed in from everywhere. What good was having a plastic bookstore bag sale and exchange concern if they didn't have the time to go to bookstores anymore? From a modest, small enterprise they very smoothly went multinational. It was time to find subcontractors and to keep only the most difficult cases for themselves, the rarest prospecting trips.

Chapter 15

Love at First Sight
in a Suburban Train

At six in the evening, Hortense met Laurie at her Main Headquarters at L'Imperial Sentier qui Bifurque café. They ordered two Guinness drafts and dove with sheer delight into the brown and not too cold froth of this divine drink. Between her first and second Guinness, Laurie recommended a few things to Hortense, which we will promptly summarize because time is short, not even twenty-four hours having gone by since the novel started and we're already at chapter 15; this is not the moment to surrender to the joys of sharply transcribing dialogue. There were three chief recommendations, one internal and two external, in the following order:

I. You do what you want;

II. Resume your philosophy studies, therefore go to the library;

III. Beginning tomorrow Sunday (it was therefore a Saturday, as you might well have suspected. Why?), pay a call on her Aunt Aspasie, in the suburbs, in Sainte-Brunehilde-les-Forêts.

Aunt Aspasie indeed

a) exists;

b) is deaf, and doesn't answer the phone.

Why go see Aunt Aspasie? Because it may serve a purpose.

And so Sunday, the following day, in the early afternoon, Hortense was on the suburban train that was going to conduct her to Aunt Aspasie's in Sainte-Brunehilde-les-Forêts.

She was never to arrive (careful, you've got the wrong idea: it's not in this chapter that Hortense is abducted; it's still too soon).

When she had announced the previous evening at dessert that "my friend, tomorrow I'm going to Aunt Aspasie's," her husband said nothing, but he raised his eyebrows and his face took the suspicious expression Hotello had in front of his dish when, beneath the obvious mackerel, he senses the surreptitious vegetable.

The suburban train for Sainte-Brunehilde-les-Forêts was a double-decker hybrid of an orange train-steamship and high speed line. Hortense found a seat in the front on the upper deck of the first car, where the scenery can be best seen, and took out of her plastic bookstore bag from Barcelona (a gift from Laurie) the third volume of Hegel's *Logic* and *Stanze* by Giorgio Agamben (in the original language, Etruscan) and got ready for an excellent afternoon.

They left the City between two enormous rows of black high rises and they headed for the suburbs between two rows of black high rises, only not as high. Abandoned factories came into view, then "Durand Helical Gearing" signs, small suburban bungalows of dirty brick, vegetable gardens full of cinders. They crossed the river with a peninsula where peaceful asparagus grows under the stinking irrigation of the sewers. A powerful reek of burnt rubber passed through the car. In short, the scenery.

They stopped at Bacon-les-Mouillères. A man in black took a seat on the other side of the compartment, aisle side. He brought out of his pocket a small green-covered volume of the Loeb Classical Library. It was Sextus Empiricus (Greek text on the left). The gentleman was Inspector Arapède. Arapède was tailing Hortense. She did not suspect it.

Less than a minute afterward, a young man came into the compartment. He sat opposite Hortense.

In these high speed-steamer-suburban trains, as everyone knows, the compartments are rather narrow. There you are in your seat, your legs out in front of you and if somebody's across from you and likewise has his legs out in front (that is, he is not a legless cripple or stretched out on the seat in defiance of the regulations), it is extremely difficult to avoid foot, leg and knee contact. This is something Hortense came to see very quickly.

She had not looked up from her book when the young man had taken his seat, enthralled as she was by the description that Giorgio Agamben gives of the "demon of melancholy," the "meridian demon" which makes the sun appear pitch black in the sky and seduces you with the drug of despair. But feeling a knee entanglement of sorts she raised her eyes and

*   *   *

she raised her eyes and
was struck right to her heart.

In a Peter Greenway film, which you've certainly seen, a few Englishmen tell about their experience of being "struck by lightning" and surviving. If he had known Hortense, there is no doubt whatsoever he would have added her to his collection. At the time she really thought she would not survive: her heart raced, slowed down, her brain melted like a lamb's brain in a butter-lemon sauce, she felt hot and cold all over in places I can't mention, she felt herself shivering, wobbling, trembling. She was struck by love at first sight.

When she was more or less sure of surviving this storm of her senses she glanced in the window to look at what had caused her insides to be thrown into such turmoil: she saw a Handsome Young Man, whose features were at once strangely familiar and imprecise. The magnet of his eyes turned away slightly, attracting the filings of Hortense's gaze.

All of this happened in the deepest silence. The only sound that could be heard was the train grating on its switches. The train stopped at a station, left again, suburban bungalows followed upon suburban bungalows and Hortense's knees were more and more entangled with the young man's, her glances intertwined with his.

The train stopped at Sainte-Brunehilde-les-Forêts. The train waited patiently at Sainte-Brunehilde-les-Forêts for Hortense kindly to collect her thoughts and her plastic bag and get off to pay her call on her Aunt Aspasie. Hortense did not move. With a sigh the train set off again. The station flashed past our eyes:

Sainte-Brunehilde-les-Forêts   Sainte-Brunehilde-les-Forêts   Sainte-Brunehilde-les-Forêts   Sainte-Brunehilde-les-Forêts   Sainte-Brunehilde-les-Forêts   Sainte-Brunehilde-les-Forêts   Sainte-Brunehilde-les-Forêts, said the signposts flashing past faster and faster and less and less legibly as the train, sighing, gained speed to make up for lost time.

"You missed your station, Mademoiselle," said the young man politely.

Hortense looked at him in disbelief. That voice. That voice. It wasn't possible. It was. It was Morgan (Prince Gormanskoï, as we know). As if he had guessed she was about to utter his name, he shushed her with his left index finger on his lips (vertically). (I must in truth say that this sign has a quite different meaning in Poldevian, which Hortense was perfectly familiar with. She blushed.)

"Maybe we can get off at the next one. There's a train in the other direction in thirty-seven minutes."

The following station was Saint-Gabriel-sur-Seigle. It was located, like Sainte-Brunehilde-les-Forêts, at the edge of the forest but at the other end. Stepping onto the platform, Hortense experienced a slight weakness and dizzy spells and Morgan (the prince) suggested that she rest a moment at the station café to recover. There was no sign of Arapède on the horizon.

They went into the train station café where they drank lemonades, silently. Then Morgan suggested going back to Sainte-Brunehilde through the forest, slowly; the air would do her good. Hortense consented.

The forest was green and thick and dark. A path disappeared into the undergrowth in the direction of Sainte-Brunehilde. At the verge of the woods there was a sign:

YOU ARE ENTERING A FOREST. BE CAREFUL!
ONE TREE CAN HIDE ANOTHER!

They entered the forest. They did not speak. They held hands. There were small variously colored flowers. Hortense gathered small variously colored flowers and put them in her hair where they did not stay. Her heart, her senses, her brain were simmering a little less; they were gradually getting used to this new, implausible, impossible, real situation.

They crossed through the forest. They still were not speaking. They arrived in Sainte-Brunehilde, but they didn't go toward Aunt Aspasie's small house. They got on a train heading back to the City. They stopped at Bacon-les-Mouillères. They got off. An enormous, almost blind building facade loomed over the tracks. It read: Flaubert Hotel. They went in. The female proprietor, with one eye missing and the other crossed, handed them the key for room 37 along with a towel. They went up. The room was on the third floor, and had a single window with dirty curtains looking out on the tracks. Trains passed in both directions.

"Take off your clothes," said Morgan.

"You first," said Hortense.

And thus on this waning Sunday afternoon, in the Flaubert Hotel, in a room that was at once sordid and sublime, Hortense committed Adultery (that's how it's said; according to the survey I made, only 6 percent of the people questioned by polling organizations know the meaning of that word).

That evening, Hortense served peas for dinner. Her husband

bid her good night and left for his job on the *Newspaper*. Hortense went into her bedroom. The six stuffed koalas waited for her like good bears on the piano. They cast her a nasty look; all except one, the softest, the most cuddly, her favorite. She took it with her to bed, hugged it against her breast and fell asleep.

While sleeping, she dreamed of Gormanskoï, of her lover Morgan. As on that afternoon in the Flaubert Hotel, she leaned over him and kissed on his left buttock the Trademark of the Poldevian Princes, the snail.

But the small dots sprinkling it were not in their places!

Chapter 16

The Cross-examination of the Bells

After Sunday, exclusively consecrated to the torrid passion of Hortense, our heroine, and Gormanskoï-Morgan, we must on Monday get back to the investigation of Balbastre's murder, which hasn't made all that much progress until now.

On Monday morning, Arapède is in a bad mood. Absorbed in reading about the paradox of the pupil in Lucian of Samosata, he let Hortense get off at Saint-Gabriel-sur-Seigle and wound up in Saint-Cucufa. (The paradox is truly quite something indeed, and Arapède's fascination is understandable: a famous lawyer has a disciple, to whom he is teaching the art of making speeches for the defense. "When will I pay you, Master?" said the pupil. "When you win your first trial." Shortly afterward, the pupil declared himself ready to start his career and announced at the same time to the teacher that under no circumstances would he pay him. "What's that," said the teacher, "you must pay me as soon as you win your first trial. Do you think then that you'll never win?" "No," said the pupil, "but I will not pay you." The furious teacher served a writ on him. But here is the Paradox: if the teacher wins, the pupil must pay him but he has lost his first trial, therefore he owes him nothing. If the pupil wins, he doesn't have to pay, but he has won his first trial, therefore he must pay. In each case, there is a contradiction which Arapède mentally licked his chops over to the point of forgetting about his shadowing.)

On Monday morning, Blognard was happy. The day before,

Madame Blognard had made her first spring stew. She used the famous chef Pierre Lartigue's recipe, presented in the form of a six stanza poem with an envoi, a sestina. The result was sheer perfection and Blognard tackled the week's work in an excellent frame of mind.

This Monday morning, Blognard and Arapède interrogated the two bell ringers, Crétin Guillaume and Molinet Jean. The interrogation took place on the spot, in the belfry, the two individuals unable to leave it in order to go to Blognard's office, Quay of Entry-into-the-Matter, because they had to ring each hour and each half hour. They shared the bell ringers' Sainte-Gudule apartment, which went with the position, located in the belfry one floor below the bells. It was reached by a spiral staircase made up of seventy-three steps.

Before climbing, Blognard dropped in at Madame Groichant's to buy four pairs of butter croissants for each of the four protagonists of the interrogation session. It was more comfortable.

Madame Groichant was at the cash register, doing her best to disregard the intense stares of the Handsome Young Man, her new pastry boy, who was assiduous in his attentions. She liked him very much, found him pretty (he resembled, she thought, her favorite singer, who had been her mother's favorite too: Jean Sablon), but she remained steadfast, now displaying in her defense a brioche's supple resistance, now the cold impermeability of a sugar frosting. The boy said his name was Stéphane. When Blognard came into the bakery he was singing the rest of the song "The Linzer Torte," whose text you read in chapter 12, paragraph 7:

> Plum pie
> In Pampelune
> Takes on a cat piss tint
> But in Mayence

It's earthenware
That gives its dull hue

Napoleons
Near Argenteuille
Take on an undefinable tint
But in Monceau-les-Mines
It's baking flour
That gives its sandy hue

Cream puffs
In Bohemian Moravia
Take on a socialist tint
But in the Ukraine
It's porcelain
That gives its hue of schist

Pear pie
In the douars
Takes on a rubbishy tint
But in Brisbane
It's propane
That gives its hue of brick

Sweet potato pie
In the Carpathians
Takes on a bloody tint
But in Cabourg
It's Loo-oove
That gives its hue of phlegm

After the sixth stanza you generally pause a moment to
catch your breath. So shall we.

At the moment he was leaving the store Blognard heard
that Stéphane had changed songs. He now was addressing
himself directly to Madame Groichant, who looked at once
offended and flattered while hearing the first verse of

"Stéphane the Pastry Boy's Song"

My heart is filled
With frangipane
You looked at me
And it fell down

Refrain:
Make no mistake, you're aiming
Straight for my poor heart's filling.

.　.　.

The belfry was rectangular. It was twelve yards six inches long approximately and approximately six yards six and three-quarters inches wide. The bell ringers' apartment was one single room with a corner kitchen and a small, comfortable bathroom, almost square-shaped: six yards three inches approximately by six yards six and three-quarters inches or so. A very steep and narrow flight of steps provided access to the floor above where the bells were located. The room was very sparsely furnished.

Crétin Guillaume and Molinet Jean were each seated at opposite ends of the room. They resembled each other like two monozygotic drops of water, and were each a Handsome Young Man. The interrogation was a doubles Ping-Pong match of sorts in which the two teams were inwardly antagonists: Molinet Jean and Arapède on one side of the net, Blognard with Crétin Guillaume on the other.

When the two inspectors came in, the two ringers were watching their TV which was running an interview with Dew-Pon Dew-Val: Tom Butler, in response to a reporter's question, revealed that the stunning success of their group in Poldevia came from the fact that his, Tom Butler's, grandmother was Poldevian. "And she was a saintly woman," he added while nodding his pretty head.

Interrogation Notes
(excerpted from Arapède's notebook)

Place of birth: Mons (Athys- for Molinet Jean, -en-Baroeul for Crétin Guillaume).
Nationality: Burgonian (passport furnished to this effect; seemed authentic).
Birth: the same day.
Blognard: You're twins?
Arapède: You're twins?
Molinet Jean and Crétin Guillaume (*together*): Yes.
Blognard: But you don't have the same name.
Molinet Jean: No; nor the same father.
Crétin Guillaume: Nor the same mother.
Arapède: And yet you're twins?
Molinet Jean: Yes.
Crétin Guillaume: Yes.
Blognard: How do you explain this fact?
Molinet Jean and Crétin Guillaume (*together*): We can't explain it, it's one of the mysteries of existence.

Arapède (*to Crétin Guillaume*): 3 + 7
Answer: 4
Arapède (*to the same*): 7 + 3
Answer: 1
Arapède (*to Molinet Jean*): 9 + 14
Answer: 5
Arapède (*to the same*): 14 + 9
Answer: 5
Arapède (*to both*): 18 + 19
Both: 1
Arapède (*to both*): 19 + 18
Answer: 10

Blognard (*to both*): Can you play for us the thirty-three

strokes of midnight, the way you played them that night between Friday and Saturday?

Together: Do re mi fa sol la la do sol re fa mi mi la fa do re sol sol me re la do fa fa sol do mi la re re fa la

"Did you know the victim?"

"Oh, he was a good fellow, always in a good mood, always lovey-dovey when he would come with his master to play organ."

Alibis:
Moliet Jean: in his bed.
Crétin Guillaume: in his bed.
Witnesses?
Molinet Jean: Crétin Guillaume.
Crétin Guillaume: Molinet Jean.

Chapter 17

Nasty Little Bugs
in the Programs

While coming down the spiral stairs Blognard said to Arapède, "Didn't you notice anything odd?"

"No, what?"

"I didn't see any bats. Did you see any bats?"

"No, I didn't see any bats."

"Yet there are always bats in a belfry. Especially in a belfry as frightening as this one" (frightening because of the thirty-three strokes of midnight that immediately preceded Balbastre's murder).

Shortly afterward, Blognard said, "Well, then, your conclusions?"

"They are no more Burgonian than I am."

"And that wasn't the only thing they lied about."

"Yes, I noticed there wasn't a single *si* in their bell melody. And *si*, in Poldevia, is the note of truth. Now, they count and perform arithmetical operations in the Poldevian manner. I therefore think that they are Poldevian and that they're lying."

"That's my feeling too," said Blognard. "But what are they hiding?"

Blognard went next to Madame Eusèbe's where we saw Jim Wedderburn buying yogurt. Eusèbe was in bed with the beautiful twins (not twin maidens! How twisted your mind is! Did you study under Q-isn't-that-so and Reckless Disregard, or what?), the beautiful twin *lenses* of his field glasses, his binoculars. He was laid up by his rheumatism and Madame Eusèbe had installed a mirror to allow him, with his binoculars, to look at tourists passing by in the street. He was filled with excitement by the apparent proximity of the forms he discovered before his eyes (as a matter of fact, it was around this time he decided not to get out of bed anymore). Madame Eusèbe was ill at ease. She told how she discovered the body. Her yellow cat, big and stupid, was now limping around on two paws; he had not wanted to admit his defeat before Hotello, who must have given him a new thrashing. Blognard did not ask Madame Eusèbe any indiscreet questions; he merely remained silent one long, very long minute (lasting exactly seventy-three seconds), riveting her with an absent-minded air. Finally, she could hold out no longer:

"It's not Alexandre Vladimirovitch, Chief Inspector, I swear. It's not him!"

"But who said it was Alexandre Vladimirovitch, Madame?" said Blognard in a very gentle voice.

She knew nothing, he was certain, and he left her there.

The time had come to go back to the office and consult the computer. The principle was simple: Blognard would ask the computer for a list of all persons who had had run-ins, recent or not (but it wouldn't go back farther than World War II), with dogs; there would be all the known dog molesters, with their methods, cases of attacked or murdered dogs, recent or unresolved . . . He didn't really think it would produce any earthshaking results, but an effort had to be made.

In the hallway before arriving at the office, they met the Poldevian inspector She. Hol. who was coming out of the men's room. The men's room was located between Blognard's office and the room with the computer which Blognard could consult thanks to a terminal and screen placed on his desk. Inspector She. Hol. followed them into the office. He came in and said:

"My name is Shorulikeszaky Hilumosedjydja. ....
...."

It took a while. Arapède translated.

"The inspector brings it to your attention that the men's room of your Quay of the Entry-into-the-Matter is far from spotless. In my country, the cleanliness of toilets is given great attention. There is a saying in my country which goes: 'The cleanliness of toilets is next to Godliness.' I taught my son how to behave properly with this toilet problem. He's five, but he never forgets to wipe around the rim of the basin after using it. Human beings in your land are really selfish. Can't they acknowledge the responsibility for these 'things' that come out of them? Don't they have any thought for the person who cleans the filthy toilets? Is this what's called culture? The other day I was standing in line in front of the door to the toilets at a department store and I heard an enormous paper-sound coming from inside. And yet the person who came out was a young and elegant woman. In my country, my son, who is six, knows that he mustn't make any noise when going to stool and he flushes silently."

Blognard made no answer to this speech but headed toward his terminal. He answered the inspector's question that he was hoping to obtain a few clues by consulting the list of dog molesters. And the inspector began with these words:

"I see clearly and I am honored to witness a demonstration of the scientific methods of the great Blognard, our model. There's nothing like the scientific method. Not long ago, my son, who is six years old, told me: 'Papa, yesterday I farted in the bathtub. At first, I smelled the bubbles as they came up to the surface. But afterwards I trapped them in a bowl and then smelled them. Well, it stank exactly the same.' I think my son will be a great scientist, don't you?"

Inspector Blognard made no answer but, sitting down before his computer screen, he started up the search program for the list he desired. There were a few crackles and whines and before his eyes

*　　*　　*

these words appeared on the screen:

Pachelbel: *Hexacordum Apollinis*, Aria Sebaldina.

and at the same time, from the depths of the computer emerged the deep and solemn sound of organ music.

The Poldevian inspector, Inspector Blognard, and Inspector Arapède remained speechless, petrified by sudden shock, like three statues of rock salt.

Without waiting for them to regain their senses, let's make a sudden leap backwards to the neighborhood of Sainte-Gudule. At the moment when Blognard was leaving Madame Eusèbe to get back to his office, Père Sinouls was crossing the threshold of the Hotel of the Poldevian Ambassadors, where the offices of the Center for Comparative Patanalysis were located, which housed his computer. He was coming to work. He had needed almost forty-eight hours to span this short distance, since he had already made the decision to work after his session of Beeranalysis with Hortense in chapter 13. The reason was that he needed some consolation to get over Balbastre's death. He had gone to the Gudule Bar. Madame Yvonne offered him a beer; Monsieur Yvonne, Arsène, had come up from the cellar and offered him a Finnish beer that he had just received; he returned the politeness; it added up to quite a few beers, and he had gone home to meditate. The following day, going to the office was out of the question, it being Sunday, and what's more the condolences were streaming in and his family was back.

Just under the offices of the Center was a coffee-roasting

shop and the aroma of Arabica and Colombia deeply permeated the atmosphere. Père Sinouls found it stimulating. He turned on the computer: the screen lit up with a soft amber glow, at once elegant, reassuring, sober and seductive. He felt really perked up. Having called up his "menu" and playing for a moment chasing a few signs in the corner of the screen with the different animals of his word processing menagerie (there was a hopping kangaroo, a raccoon for cleaning house, a cat for insertions, a giraffe for going into corners, etc.), a matter of limbering up his fingers, he set about moving on to more serious things.

He had to try the section of the program he had written Friday, before the incident. He took it out of his shirt and his undershirt, looked at it, frowned: he didn't remember what it was about anymore. A title was indeed marked, but he drew an absolute blank. In addition, there was something that was obviously not working in the program; something was missing; a small function, yes, there was a small function he had jotted down somewhere, on a scrap of paper. He opened the drawer and felt a pang of anguish. All these scraps of paper with small functions! How can he find the right one? "This damned memory of mine," he thought, "I've absolutely got to cut out the booze."

Finally, all was ready. Sinouls placed himself in front of the screen, whose beautiful amber glow always gave him joy. He had discovered the color and material necessary for his screen during a trip to London that Madame Sinouls had dragged him on, since she wanted to see the new Turner "disposition" at the Clore Gallery. Fortunately there were the pubs! It was in a display cabinet at the Victoria and Albert Museum that he spotted the piece of amber. He had immediately demanded that his computer screen be an exact imitation of its texture, polish, luminosity and charm. It had cost the Center for Comparative Patanalysis a small fortune. There were a few rumbles and groans in the electronic bowels, then a triumphant beep and the "beast," as Sinouls would affectionately call it, said:

"I am ready."

Sinouls inserted his diskette and waited. On the screen appeared a list of names with a few explanatory lines. Dumbfounded, and pulling closer to see better, Sinouls read the following:

Orsells, Philibert, philosopher.
Method of approaching dogs: sits in a square and begins reading excerpts from his recent works in front of a dog he has chosen as his victim. When the unfortunate creature, unable to take any more, makes a motion to bite, he lodges a complaint against the owner and demands that the dog be destroyed.

Appalled and incredulous, Sinouls started up his printer, which immediately ran out a list of dog molesters in the City, the very one that Blognard had not received, who instead was treated to some organ music. We know the criminal had switched the two diskettes so as to delay the inspector's search. But as for Sinouls, he had no idea what was going on.

At first he thought that it was some bugs up to their tricks, those little creatures lodging in programs, software, diskettes and circuits, and whose chief activity consists in disrupting them, tangling them up, eating and deteriorating them completely. The ambition of their species is to create a sufficient disorder in the computers of the Great Global Powers so as to trigger by mistake the war that will rid them of human beings and allow them to hold undivided dominion over the planet.

Another bug, thought Sinouls in the beginning. But at once a cold sweat covered him. He had just remembered that in his new language, a recent secret invention of Professor Girardzoï called LAPEFALL (Language to Put an End Finally to All Languages), *it was no longer possible* for a mistake to be introduced; *the program verified itself* and automatically gunned down all the bugs.

What had happened?

He rushed to his LAPEFALL manual.

The manual had vanished!

Chapter 18

One of the Author's Secrets

Responding to Inspector Blognard's summons, I arrived just in time to witness the stupefaction of these three honorable detectives, but not soon enough to understand the reason. From Blognard's terminal there arose organ music, and their stillness looked to the world like a homage rendered to the divine persuasion of the *Hexacordum Apollinis*.

Blognard let the first variation come to an end, then shut the computer off. Silence reigned. No one said anything. No explanation was given for what I had just heard. By mutual agreement they put off their exclamations of surprise for a later time. It is solely because, being the Author, I necessarily *knew* that something unusual had just happened that I was able to take note of their sangfroid despite the fact something unusual had just happened. Blognard acted as if everything was going "according to plan" in the most orderly and routine of investigations. I had quite willingly obeyed the inspector's summons because I wished to examine up close, and in action, Blognard's new gadget, his terminal and screen with his latest version of the Mac Alpine word processor and the Detective software that had just been made available to him. But in spite of everything, I wondered what he really could want from me.

He told me that he wished to have my opinion at this important moment of the investigation, and especially at this important moment in my novel which described the events necessitating the investigation, because it had reached the midway point.

I understood at once that I was under suspicion. Perhaps I'm exaggerating a little. He did not really suspect me, but he did not entirely eliminate the hypothesis that I could be mixed up in this affair in a more direct, more intimate way than by simply being his scribe, his storyteller.

Blognard's dealings with literature were not very extensive. He barely had the time to read, and he read chiefly those classics that Madame Blognard recommended to him. Thus he was extremely wary of modern literature. And he did not realize that there wasn't the slightest chance that my book would be one of those incongruous avant-gardist variations of the detective novel: the kind in which the *Author* is the culprit. We have seen the Detective as Criminal, as Victim, the Narrator as Culprit, every combination has been tried, but the novel has yet to be written in which the Reader is the culprit, or the one in which he is the Victim; nor has any attempt been made to drag the Author into these perverse fantasies. At any rate, these gimmicks aren't going to start with me. Even if I had been able, for reasons of theoretical experimentation which are, I repeat, totally foreign to the high idea I hold of the novelist's duties, to envisage for one second being Balbastre's murderer, I most certainly would not have followed through. Finding it even more painful to be in other bodies than in my own, I would have swiftly renounced the idea.

Blognard's questions confirmed my hypothesis. He asked me, skillfully and hypocritically taking an interest in my work habits, what I had done on the night of the crime, and I understood that he wanted to verify that I had an alibi.

Indeed I did.

I had gone over to Laurie and Carlotta's for my weekly TV evening. I had watched all in a row Super Jaimie, Mr. Spock, my favorite hero in "Star Trek," Kit the Car (a heroine whose voice is dubbed by a man), then Peter Falk in "Columbo" (my favorite hero: he has exactly the same raincoat as I do and he asks suspects questions exactly as I would like to, if I were a detective, and not an extraterrestrial with a logical mind and no emotions. The captain asks me: "The Gondwanians' force field is right in front of us. If we approach by the Brewsterian angle of incidence, what are the chances of passing through by simple refraction?" Without a moment's hesitation I answer: "One chance in 1,674,018, to be exact." The captain: "I'll take that chance." In such crucial circumstances, where the fate of the Human Race is threatened by the totalitarian Gondwanians, the Columbo method is unusable. But I would have liked to have been able to try it out on a few of the characters of the present story, like Madame Groichant's pastry boy, for example, or Molinet Jean, or Tom Butler. I am forbidden to do so, I cannot step out of my role).

Calm and collected, I answered Blognard's questions. The one I most feared never came. When I said I also watched the music program "The Thirty-Nine Steps," his interest had already waned. He knew that my alibi would hold up. So he didn't ask me why I, a novelist, would have an interest in such a musical program. And I was not all that keen on being asked the question. For it related to my *project*.

I'm going to reveal it to you in the following chapter, the first of the second half of the book. But beforehand, as an indispensable background for the elucidation of the motives behind the *project*, I must give you the following excerpts from my correspondence with the Publisher.

*　*　*

More excerpts from the (unpublished) correspondence
between the Author and the Publisher
concerning the novel entitled Our Beautiful Heroine

Ninth letter from the Author to the Publisher

Dear Publisher,

In anticipation of my book's publication by your House, I had subscribed to the totality of French and foreign periodicals so as not to risk missing the reviews that would not fail to appear on my Work and to be in a position to immediately answer by an express, personal registered letter acknowledging receipt for each one, in the shortest possible time.

As an extra precaution, I had also subscribed (at great cost) to a racket whose specialty was tracking down, clipping and forwarding reviews and mere mentions, so as to be certain of having finally at my disposal every single allusion, however minimal, to my novel.

Six weeks have gone by. The first New Zealand magazines began to reach me: two of the three rooms of my apartment on Square des Grands Edredons are already full, and I had to take refuge in the third. I must personally wait every day for the mailman to pass, since my concierge refuses henceforth to bring up the mail to my door. And yet, in the large notebook that I set aside especially for the collation of all the press clippings classified by country and date, with weight given to the importance of the publication, a weight calculated in accordance with the best specialists (following Father Risolnus's Rhythm Theory), the absolute sum total is still only *six* items. I did indeed say *six*. (My favorite is still the beautiful article, the first one, from the *Indépendant des Côtes Sud du Minervois Nord*, the terms of which I've already communicated to you [out of jealousy, no doubt, the *Moniteur des Côtes Nord du Minervois Sud* did not even make mention of the book's publication. What pettiness].) Furthermore, I have received countless dispatches (all billed to me) from the specialized agency previously mentioned, but in fact they are references to a work on *Heroin*, published in Monaco (an Andorran translation is in progress and the rights have already been bought by Lichtenstein and San Marino), a work that I have not authored and which holds as much interest for me as my first galley proofs. A quick calculation tells me that less than 0.00000001 percent of the journalistic material has thus been devoted to my book. I am appalled.

After much thought, I arrived at the following conclusion: a big splash must be made. Here's what I propose: thanks to your connections in television, you organize, rather quickly (summer is nearing!), a program at 8:30 in the evening, a debate on all channels devoted to the following question: Are Hortense's buttocks, or are they not, perfectly perfect, according to the definition of perfection given in my book by the character who is in love with Hortense? The question (and here's the clever part) would not be put to literary critics, nor to several pontificating buttockologists, but to heavyweight public figures: Raymond Barre, François Mitterand, Ronald Reagan, Margaret Thatcher, Monsignor Fustiger and—last but not least—Madame Gorbachev.

If you move promptly and decisively in this direction, victory is ours!

Cordially,

The Author

To be complete, I include the *one and only answer* from my Publisher to the thirty-seven letters that I sent him during these crucial months before the world's indifference discouraged me.

*Letter (One and Only, therefore #1) from
the Publisher to the Author*

Dear Author,

I am no longer surprised by your surprise: after an inquiry, I have no choice but to note that you are right: there are quite a few books other than your own in the bookstores! Having myself applied the Monte Carlo method, I have indeed noted that parasitical works still crowd the shelves. After having brought together the National Publishers' Union, the Society of Men of Letters, the Book Laborers and an Oulipian subset at the Writers' Center, I am in a position to furnish you with a *rational* explanation for this appalling blunder: the books you see in the bookstores are COUNTERFEITS! Very skillfully imitated counterfeits, of course, but *counterfeits!*

Your book is, alas, involved in one of the most gigantic publishing circle ploys since displaying the complete works of Rex Stout in a chic bookstore on Rue Charles-V. The entire profession has organized itself to permanently confuse the members of literary prize committees: it's a question of proving *scientifically* that this year the prizes will be awarded to a *counterfeit work*. The mechanism is simple: each participant prints his own books under another label and vice versa. Simple, isn't it? Examine the works carefully: they belong to Seuil yet bear the Gallimard imprint. Or to Grasset yet come out at Michel Albin's. This explains how certain of our colleagues have used our label to publish their works, and thus the horrible doubt that was able to creep into your mind: "My publisher is publishing books other than my own!"

Rest assured, your book is indeed the only REAL book of the present publishing season. [. . .]

[. . .] Always bear in mind this assurance: all the works not your own that you see are COME-ONS (very often, there is nothing on the inside). But if, by mistake, a few bookstores were not to sell *Our Beautiful Heroine*, you would be advised to bring it to my attention: they are in *danger*. The scheme risks being laid bare through their mistake, for *Our Beautiful Heroine* alone lends credibility to the present publishing season.

The hypocrite! (*Author's note*)

Part Four

Escape

Chapter 19

The Thirty-Nine Steps

As you may suspect, dear Reader, my first novel did not have the absolute clear-cut success I had counted on. And far from bringing me enormous sums, it even cost me very dearly: I had to pay not only for my subscriptions to numerous publications and (unjustified) bills from the agency responsible for locating mentions of my work, but I also had to settle up for all the books damaged during my run-ins with certain bookstore owners.

Upon coming out of my serious depression, I bravely resumed my work. I undertook this second novel that you are reading to give myself another chance; and also because it was an old habit.

But at the same time I told myself: "Jacques Roubaud, you mustn't put all your eggs in one basket." And I was struck by an insight that led me to my project.

One day while taking my geometry lesson, and simultaneously listening to the radio and following multiple TV programs, while Carlotta carried on with Hotello's training (which I will get to in due time), first giving demonstrations on various obstacles (chairs, rulers and armchairs), I caught by chance a glimpse of the famous musical show "The Thirty-Nine Steps."

A brief reminder of the idea behind it: every day, the songs presented to the avid public compete with each other on this program, by far the most popular of all televised shows of its kind. The songs are ranked by order of public preference (measured according to the most sophisticated survey techniques). The singers of the groups place themselves according to their rank on the thirty-nine steps of a giant staircase where at leisure they can be gazed upon, and heard, along with their music videos. The humblest are on the first step (there can be some ties), the day's winners are on the thirty-ninth and last step. So far, nothing very original in relation to the standard methods of presentation. In addition, each day the preceding day's ranking can be modified. But, and here lies the great originality of the show, a group placed on the fourteenth step, for example, and due to be relegated by the surveys to the eighteenth position in order to be replaced by the group that was previously occupying the twenty-third, is perfectly able to *refuse to give up its position* and to defend it tooth and nail (a certain number of weapons are banned) against those whom it takes for intruders. Glorious battles result, broadcast like all the rest, which have the advantage of reinforcing the athletic qualities of the singers, who are in great need of it.

My project can be summarized in one sentence: *find a way to get on "The Thirty-Nine Steps."* Such was the dazzling image that, on that day, crossed my mind. I saw myself gradually scaling the steps, with songs that were more and more beautiful and gained a vaster and vaster public vote, driven by success and training to get into impeccable condition, which would allow me to resist every assault and to progress irresistibly toward the summit.

I needed:

—to write songs,

—to try them out before an expert,

—to exercise and watch my diet.

Such was the first phase of my project.

I set myself to the task at once. My first song was the one I put into the mouth of Madame Groichant's pastry boy, Stéphane: "The Linzer Torte." I have already presented you six verses (there are sixty-three). Here are three more, such as I sang them to Carlotta, my expert:

Verses 7, 8 and 9 of the Author's Song
entitled "The Linzer Torte"

Madeleines
In the Caspian
Take on a mineral tint
But in Ireland
It's pitchblend
That gives its palish hue

Cream buns
In the Rocky Mountains
Take on a mayonnaise tint
But in New York
It's pure pork
That gives its chairy hue

Kugelhoff
In Malakoff
Takes on a volatile tint
But in Harlem
It's coffee with cream
That gives its twilight hue.

I sang it with conviction, to a melody of Mozart that I had chosen for its rousing quality. I fell silent and awaited the verdict.

Carlotta was, while listening to me, simultaneously watching the commercial with the young man in jeans on TV (these images have remained engraved in my memory), but she listened to me attentively until the end.

Her verdict was clear. She said it simply, without seeking to dissemble the truth: "It's too medieval."

My heart dropped a notch in my chest. I understood that it would be a long road.

I am still persevering.

. . .

For the sake of truth, my only guide, I ought to say that appearing on "The Thirty-Nine Steps" was only one part of my project. There was another, loftier and vaster still, and I am forced to reveal it, for it explains my relationship with Jim Wedderburn; otherwise I would know him only indirectly, something not much to my liking. I prefer to have direct *human* relationships with my characters. We aren't merely paper beings, damn it.

In the second part of my project, having earned enormous sums with my songs thanks to my success on "The Thirty-Nine Steps" (under Carlotta's monitoring, who was already training Hotello, my success, sooner or later, was assured), I would be able to invest in

THE MOVIES

I would finance a film entitled:

THE LIFE OF JACQUES ROUBAUD

I would be the film's producer, but I wouldn't act in it myself nor would I be the director. For the role of Jacques Roubaud, I see only one possibility:

with ROBERT MITCHUM as
Jacques Roubaud

There remained getting a director interested. Laurie introduced me to her colleague, Jim Wedderburn, a Handsome Young Man.

Jim Wedderburn had no small experience in the movies. He had been an actor: an American director, struck by his staggering resemblance to the young Shakespeare, had hired him in Hollywood to play all the Shakespeare roles in Westerns (small, but quite numerous roles). The scene is almost always the same. Shakespeare, discouraged by his love for the heroine who prefers Gary Cooper, Kirk Douglas or Burt Lancaster, leaps on his horse and reaches the edge of the canyon. There, he takes off his clothes (all except his Renaissance bathing trunks), saying "To be or not to be," and dives into the rapids. Everything was going fine until this precise moment (as Jim Wedderburn showed me on the copy he had kept of the rushes of his first and only Western) when the camera could not help but film, on his left buttock while he was splashing about in the creek's torrential current, the snail-shaped trademark that he had since birth. That signaled the end of his career as a Shakespearean actor. So he was hired as a director and directed two or three Westerns a year before going home to his mews to write his novels. He liked my project, and he began to give some thought to the screenplay.

His idea was not to make a banal movie bio: first this, then that; Mitchum (in the role of Jacques Roubaud) as a child, in the schoolyard ... No. He envisaged short sequences, each strictly limited to a little more than a minute, each showing a possible (or impossible, as the case may be) life of Jacques Roubaud. And in order to demonstrate the autonomy of the sequences, each would be filmed *as an independent movie,* with credits and all that stuff. "Each of these movies must," Jim Wedderburn explained, "be as intense as the best commercials (which are even shorter), like those for Orangina, Stuyvesant Travel or the Cassegrain rabbit."

In one of my lives, for example, I would be a college teacher. The camera would show the austere facade of an institution of higher learning. Jacques Roubaud—that is, imagewise, Robert Mitchum—would enter. With his inimitable gait Mitchum would advance down a long hallway. There would be heard, from the distance, a suave voice, like the female voices in airports, that would say: "The students for Monsieur

Roubaud's course are expected in room 317." Mitchum (Roubaud) would still be advancing. The same voice would begin again: "Last call for Monsieur Roubaud's course." That would be all. Sublime.

In another sequence, dramatic this time, Jacques Roubaud would be in the grips of depression. Mitchum would be seen on a bed, in a Manhattan hotel room, gloomy, unshaven, with his melancholy dimple, surrounded by half-empty bottles of bourbon. He would pick up the phone. At the other end of the line, on the other side of the ocean (the camera would follow the path of the waves in an anguish-filled traveling shot), Père Sinouls would pick up the phone, beer in hand. He would say: "Hello." Mitchum's voice would be heard, with his inimitable inflections: "Hello, Dr. Sinouls. It's Jacques Roubaud. I'd like to have the results of my analysis."

Chapter 20

Balbastre's Funeral

Père Sinouls turns off his screen, unplugs his terminal. He doesn't understand anything, not one single thing. He goes out, lost in thought, into Rue Vieille-des-Archives, and heads for his house.

Inspector Blognard is winding up his interrogation. He continues to ask a few questions but his heart is not in it anymore. He looks at his watch. It's time. We leave in the direction of Rue des Milleguiettes.

Madame Yvonne and her husband, Arsène, accompanied by the new boy at the Gudule Bar, go out into the street. The Gudule Bar is closed for an hour.

Laurie and Carlotta come down D stairway of number 53 Rue des Citoyens. Carlotta is excused from her history class because of the circumstances. The timing is perfect: she was supposed to give an analysis of one of Charles de Gaulle's speeches. She's a bit perplexed: she thought that Charles de Gaulle was an airport. She just received an excellent grade for her résumé of a theater play she had been given to read:

"There's this guy. He doesn't believe in God. So this statue busts him in the face."

The whole neighborhood is heading for Rue des Milleguiettes.

Everyone except Madame Eusèbe, because of Alexandre Vladimirovitch. Her attitude is criticized very harshly.

Indeed it is on this morning that Balbastre is buried, in Père Sinouls's family garden.

Sewn up after the autopsy, his face retouched by the undertaker, he looks peaceful, almost joyful, in his glass coffin.

Hortense is there. Her thoughts are on Morgan, her lover. She looks at the boy from the Gudule Bar, who reminds her of Morgan, her lover. She tells herself: "I love him." She also tells herself: "What am I going to do now?"

The entire Sinouls family is around the grave. Madame Sinouls, the Sinouls girls and their friends. Marc Sinouls has come home from Poldevia where he had been on tour with his friend Kayujrmdza; they were playing Concertos for Two Viols by Monsieur de Sainte-Colombe before dazzled audiences. Marc Sinouls composed a "Balbastre's Tomb," for two viols. They are going to play it this morning, after the funeral orison that the Author will deliver. They practice assiduously in the music room of the Sinouls house. Marc yawns, it's very early for him (as for Laurie), but Kayujrmdza doesn't let him fall back to sleep. She has her saber at her side and watches over the harmony of the execution.

Two gravediggers enter. They take up their places on each side of the coffin.

First gravedigger: Who builds the sturdiest houses?

Second gravedigger: I don't know and don't give a damn.

First gravedigger: We do, idiot, gravediggers do; the houses we make last till doomsday.

They spit into their hands, grip the coffin and lower it into the grave.

Père Sinouls (*he looks at Balbastre*): Alas, poor boy. Farewell you old drunk's dog!

The Author draws near the grave. In his hands he holds the sheets of paper on which his speech is written.

•   •   •

Funeral Orison for Balbastre Sinouls

"Ladies, young ladies, dear dogs, dear cats, gentlemen, Sebastien Rouillard in his great tome:

Gymnopodes or the Nakedness of the Feet. Argued on each side by S.R. de Melun, Esquire, Lawyer for Parliament, Paris, 'At Olivier,' 1624. In-4, IIf, 326 (in fact 366) p., shelf mark Arsenal 4 BL 4526

examines the question of knowing why we walk about with shoes rather than barefooted. And he concludes that it is because, creatures of sin that we are, and nakedness suitable only for innocence, we are not able, nor willing to show the nakedness of our souls, nor for the same reason, that of our feet. And yet our brother, our friend Balbastre, walked about with his feet bare. And how much that shows the especially luminous innocence of his soul, oh how much indeed, because he had four, feet that is."

Such was the exordium of my speech which I am not reproducing in its entirety: you can read it on the Sinoulses' dining room wall, where it is displayed between Guyomard's painting *Balbastre on a Bicycle* and Getzler's, where six Balbastres in rugby uniforms clash with a Welsh pack.

The actual speech consists of six periods:

In the first, I describe Balbastre's physical beauties.

In the second, his spiritual beauties.

In the third, the union of physical and spiritual beauties, which the notion of canineness sheds light upon. I relate in this regard how on certain Sundays, having tea and cakes at the Sinoulses' while we would talk, Balbastre would place himself at my left hand and I would continuously massage his head and thorax, patting vigorously with my palm while he remained still, the very image of canineness.

In the fourth period I depicted the grief of the family.

In the fifth the particular grief of his master, Père Sinouls.

How they would go out together, Père Sinouls to buy a copy of the *Newspaper* and beer, Balbastre to piss on lampposts, hubcaps, and bushes while dreaming of his great lost love, the little bitch Voltige.

In the last period I invoked the foul black soul of the criminal, I felt him lurking around us, prey to remorse.

I did not ask for vengeance, but for justice.

Thus I held forth.

Then the noble and elegiac, tender and suggestive music, embellished with barking metaphors, of "Balbastre's Tomb" by Marc Sinouls welled up, played by the two violists before the grave, at the head of the body. He looked so alive, so peaceful that we were expecting at any moment to see him get up, shake himself off and accompany the sound of the instruments with a long howl, on the major third.

However, while I was thus delivering, before the moved and often weepy gathering, Balbastre's Funeral Orison, there happened past, invisible to all but three people, his ghost. He entered the garden, moved about among the gathering and came to sit on the other side of the grave, opposite the musicians.

Who saw him? I, you (but it has to do with the me and you who are invisibly watching the scene, not of the me who is delivering the speech) and another. You correctly guess that it's the murderer!

And Balbastre's ghost spoke:

Balbastre's ghost: There's something rotten in the neighborhood of Sainte-Gudule.

Upon hearing those fateful words, the murderer, although murderer he was and with nerves of steel, decided to slip away. Which he did. His absence, which we did not witness with our own eyes (let us make definite note of this), passed unnoticed by everybody, except Carlotta.

It was not fear that made him flee. He was intrepid. It was not remorse. What then?

If it be true, as Spinoza declares, that the concept of a dog does not bite, the ghost of a dog, no doubt, does not have the patience of a concept. And the murderer did not want to discover, at his expense, that Balbastre's could not only address his ears, but also his calves.

After the condolences, friends and family stayed behind and had a bite.

Chapter 21

A Documentary Chapter

This chapter is a break for a moment's meditation. We should:

—Meditate in memory of Balbastre;

—Consult the appended Documents:

1. The Map of the Area (see the following page);

2. The Trademarks (see the page following the following page). These are the trademarks of the Poldevian princes that can be seen on the left buttocks of the princes. They are symbolic snails;

—Seek, like Inspector Blognard, the Solution.

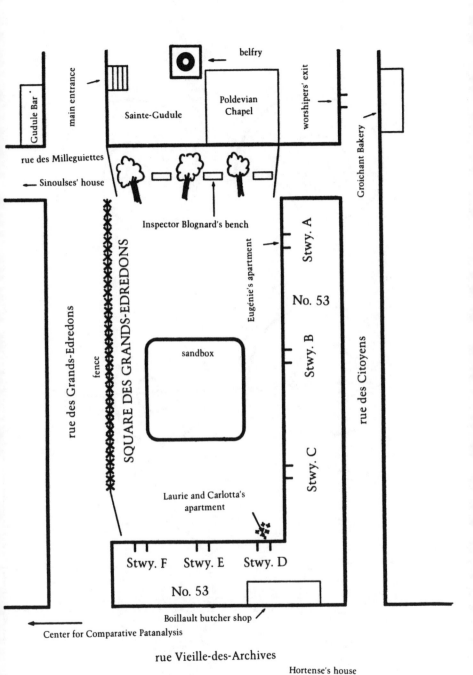

MAP OF THE AREA

Trademarks

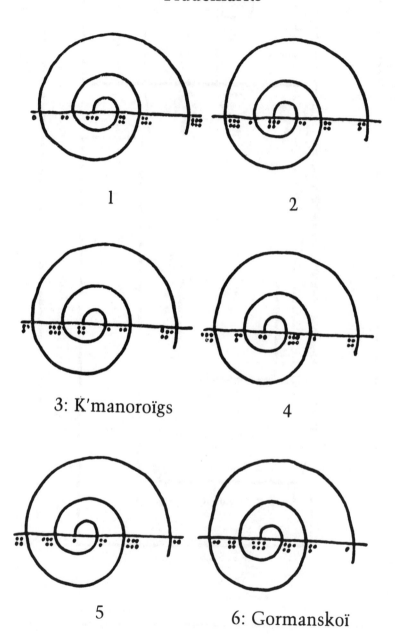

1

2

3: K'manoroïgs

4

5

6: Gormanskoï

Chapter 22

Le Marché des Bébés Orange

A few steps from Sainte-Gudule's, going northward, is located the Marché des Bébés Orange. It's a real market, the kind that has fallen out of custom. It has a real demarcated district, enclosed by walls. There are two entrance doors, above which can be read, in proudly Gothic lettering:

Marché des Bébés Orange
fondé en 1317.

It doesn't slump about wretchedly in the street, tossing its apple cores and lettuce stumps under passing cars like others I will not mention.

It has its grass merchants, its flower merchants, its merchants selling nothing at all. You hear the old-fashioned voices, as beautiful as Gregorian chants:

"Get your cucumbers here, ladies!"

"Beautiful pumpkins, step right up!"

"Don't buy over here, you'll pay less!"

When you enter, from Rue Julot, you discover on each side of the entrance two rows of babies squealing and drooling in orange rompers, backed up by au pair college girls in Playmate uniforms trying to maintain the noise level of their belches within a limit of decency by rocking the green carriages they are confined to. It's a gift from the municipality to the population. The general idea of the procedure is that tourists, reading the market's name at the entrance and plunging into their guidebooks and dictionaries in order to get their bearings, will find their deductions confirmed by this meaningful spectacle. They read: "Bébés Orange," understand "Orange Babies" or "Bimbi di colore arancio" or "Limonosoff zakouski," whatever the case may be. And just below, what do they see? Orange-colored babies wriggling about. It's one mark of the recent progress in Applied Linguistics and Communication Theory, aiming to lessen the arbitrary nature of the sign, which diminishes our share of markets in international commerce.

Contrary to the persistent legends conveyed by tourist agencies, the *name* "Marché des Bébés Orange" does not itself go back to the fourteenth century. It's a matter of a pure phonetic shift. In this covered market, livestock was once sold. There were cows, pigs, broods of chicks; goats, sheep, ewes. This last, precisely, are what the French call "brebis," and there was a certain "brebis" merchant, so the story goes, who did not master his flocks. And his group of ovines would ovinely get mixed up with the other groups who looked at them bovinely. Consequently he had put up a sign (in Gothic letters) at the entrance:

Ses brebis on range! Marché!
[Round up your ewes! March!]

You see the shift: ses brebis on range marché ses brebis on range marché ses brebis on range marché . . . brebis . . . bébé on range . . . orange. *Marché des Bébés orange.* And that's that. It is one of the beautiful examples that Philibert Orsells, our great philosopher, gives in his "etimologies."

Time leaped from Monday, Balbastre's funeral, to Saturday, market day. Laurie and Hortense are going to the Marché des Bébés Orange.

Laurie managed to drink her first cup of tea before eleven, thanks to Carlotta who brought over her croissants and the

Newspaper. It was sunny; she agrees to rise. However Hotello is in love with these two redheaded girls into whose lives, for extrinsic reasons, he chose to enter. He doesn't at all like that Carlotta (whom he loves) brings to Laurie (whom he loves, and whose pillow he occupies) croissants and brioches. He stretches out, demands his share, tries to push Carlotta out of bed, unhooks the phone (which he is fiercely jealous of) and ends up by kidnapping Laurie's wristwatch, which he takes to his stash of booty. That way she will no longer see the time and she'll miss meeting Hortense at the market and they will both stay on the pillow. By the way, I must point out to you that Alexandre Vladimirovitch, the cat once belonging to Madame Eusèbe, had been in love with a ginger cat named Tioutcha (I don't know why I'm telling you this again now: it came to me suddenly. So, before I forget . . .). Time is passing. Laurie finishes her crossword puzzle in the *Newspaper.* She gets up. Hotello is going to sulk by placing his own black against the black of the piano.

* * *

Once at the bottom of the stairs on her way out, Laurie can turn left along D, E, and F buildings, come out of the corridor separated from the square by the fence in Rue des Grands-Edredons, once more turn left in the street, then again left in Rue Vieille-des-Archives to meet up with Hortense, on the other side of the intersection, who is waiting for her outside her door, under the false acacias. But here's the problem: the co-owners suddenly and gravely afflicted by an attack of co-ownership had had installed recently a lock on the Grands-Edredons entrance so as to protect the co-owned property from infinitely pernicious and contagious non-co-owners passing through (tenants being tolerated). Each authorized person had to be provided with a key to enter or leave. The co-owned property had initially decided to put a second lock on the other side, on Rue de l'Abbé-Migne, at the end of the passage successively leading along the fence on the square to C, B, and A stairways (follow me on the map on page 135). But it hadn't been installed yet. Laurie, who had no excessive love for locks, therefore had to turn right, then right, then right, to meet up with Hortense where they had agreed. They walked part of the way along Rue Vieille-des-Archives, then along Rue Julot. Hortense, happy as a lark, was singing an old song that Morgan had taught her:

> Her health became so fragile
> One day under an automobile
> Without a thought she passed on
> And when Saint Peter opened up
> The gates of Paradise
> There he still was
> Her Big Julot

It was an appropriate choice for the occasion.

"Morgan's the one," she said, "who taught it to me."

They went to the café on the corner for Laurie's two coffees. In front of her cold milk and bread and butter, Hortense told all. Laurie did not disapprove.

Traffic was particularly heavy at the Marché des Bébés Orange. The babies were crying, more or less neglected, in their orangeades: all their nannies had rushed around Tom Butler, Carlotta's passion and crooner with Dew-Pon Dew-Val, who had come to do his food shopping. He was buying endives and signing autographs. For, contrary to what Carlotta believed based on the faulty translation from a Monegasque magazine, Dew-Pon Dew-Val did not have their recording studio in a disused dock at the port in Manchester (nor Nottingham) where Carlotta and Eugénie had planned to hang around casually in the neighboring streets during their vacation (it was the same studio for the group Hi Hi) whistling tunes while waiting for Tom Butler or Martenskoï (Eugénie's great love) to come out. Indeed, Dew-Pon Dew-Val had been recording for some while at the Hotel of the Poldevian Ambassadors, above the coffee shop and next to Père Sinouls's office.

Laurie bought a roast beef of angler salmon for lunch, and two mackerels for Hotello. She asked for a half-pound slab of salted butter, bufala mozzarella, conte, morbier, brousse and farmhouse bread at the dairy counter. Then they went over to the vegetable huckster, Madame Bette, née Carde. Madame Bette was an original seller who had perfected a sales strategy of the highest theoretical interest. According to the classic Theory (valid not only for the sale of vegetables but also for cold cuts, meat and everything that is weighed out and requires a scale), let us suppose for example that someone asks for two pounds of sweet potatoes (of so-so, theoretical sweet potatoes, quality doesn't matter): the sales-person takes a few sweet potatoes from the pile of potatoes, takes *more than two pounds* (which is easy to do once you get the knack), throws it forcefully onto the scale whose needle clearly exceeds the two pound mark. Even before the two pound mark is exceeded (no time must be allowed for the needle to move backward), you say: "There's a little more, is it OK like that?" It's OK. This system, recommended as I repeat by the classic Theory, has a certain advantage: you sell more than demand which, in principle, increases earnings. There is however one disadvantage which has been pointed out by several economists: the male (or female) customer feels, *subliminally*, that his/her hand has been forced. He wanted two pounds of sweet potatoes and he was made to buy two pounds four ounces or even two pounds eight. But at the same time he is not inclined to pay any mind to the price hike which must accompany the procedure. If two pounds of sweet potatoes, for example, costs 6 francs, adding an extra four ounces should, according to the theory, be charged 6.80 francs or even 7.10, if you dare. But you do not dare; not that the customer is able to perform the necessary calculation; such is very rarely the case. You do not dare because you've forced his hand on the weight and you gather he is suspicious. You say: "That comes to 6.60," and *you have not qualitatively improved the profit margin.*

Madame Bette, née Carde, had, on her own, invented the *Modern Theory of Sweet Potato Selling* (long before Spencer Friedman, who had nevertheless received the Nobel Prize in economics for this discovery).

The principle is simple: instead of taking more than two pounds from the pile of sweet potatoes, *you take less.* You say: "It's not quite two pounds. Is it OK?" On the buyer's side, dazzled by such a show of abnegation on the part of the merchant, the person says, subjugated: "Yes, that's fine." So far, in appearance, you are the loser. But that's the whole beauty of the system: you can then, with total peace of mind, give a little helping nudge to up the posted price without risking the slightest frown. *You sell less, but make more.* And you earn a faithful clientele.

I had, one day while I was accompanying Laurie to the market for my research, noticed Madame Bette's discovery. She had noticed that I was noticing and since then regularly served Laurie at the correct price and exact weight, which Laurie had only to be all too pleased about.

It was the day in the week Groichant's bakery was closed. Madame Groichant was doing her food shopping, accompanied by Stéphane, her new pastry boy, "a very Handsome Young Man" (Hortense and Laurie said in concert and unison). But Stéphane only had eyes for Madame Groichant. He cast enamored looks her way while whispering new verses of his song:

"Stéphane the Pastry Boy's Song"
(second verse)

Your creamy charms
Dance in my skull
They move me so much
I feel I'm in hell

Refrain:
Make no mistake, you're aiming
Straight for my poor heart's filling.

After the fruits and vegetables, Hortense and Laurie crossed Rue de Normandie to buy some Saint-Joseph's white wine that would go with the roast beef of angler salmon.

Then they took a break at the café at the corner of Rue Julot. Madame Groichant and Stéphane had placed their packages on the neighboring table. Stéphane was trying to seduce his boss's uncompromising knees, singing all the while:

You've got two knees
Two less than an ass
I'm so crazy I'm
Off to Sainte-Anne's, alas!

Refrain:
Make no mistake, you're aiming
Straight for my poor heart's filling.

Laurie's coffee had not arrived. She went up to the counter. The Poldevian inspector was there, She. Hol., who asked her how Hotello was getting on.

Chapter 23

Hotello Introduces Carlotta
to Gormanskoï

When Hortense and Laurie came back from the Marché des Bébés Orange, Carlotta was glued to her television. She was replaying a videocassette that she had put together, an anthology of Dew-Pon Dew-Val interviews, specially featuring Tom Butler. She was replaying it for the fourteenth time while awaiting the news. Learning that Tom Butler was live at the market, she felt thirty seconds of despair, but announced that she did not renounce in any way whatsoever her project of visiting the Manchester studios. Anyway, at any rate, Eugénie was supposed to go there too to get a glimpse of Martenskoï, her Love.

All the while looking at Tom Butler, Carlotta continued Hotello's training session. She had decided to prepare him for the hurdle race in the Olympics. You must not believe we are setting down this fact simply for our amusement. We are not here to amuse ourselves. The exceptional training that Hotello received during these sessions (and he was naturally very gifted) (speaking of which, let us point out that the Poldevians are especially adapted for leaping hurdles, morphologically, since their country is very mountainous) was a crucial cog in the machine of events, confounding the machinations of the criminal. Therefore mind your protests. Hotello's training consisted of leaping over bars placed higher and higher between the large room (where the TV was) and the kitchen. Carlotta displayed the greatest patience in order to improve Hotello's style and performance. When he succeeded she'd say: "Nice going, kitty." When he knocked down a bar or when his leaping style (a Fosbury mixed with some leopard) was not up to par, she'd say: "One more time, you little blockhead," and Hotello'd be so miffed that he surpassed himself. He leaped better and better but one thing made him anxious: he was afraid his back paws would grow too big. He leaped up onto the sink in the bathroom to look at himself in the mirror, but he did not manage to find out if his fears were justified.

Hortense and Laurie settled down in the kitchen in front of a glass of cool *blanc cassis* before carrying on with lunch preparations.

However the time for the news arrived. (When I think that you have not asked me why Carlotta was waiting for the TV news! You find it natural that she wait for the TV news? What indeed could make her want to watch the TV news? OK, when you've figured it out, you can skip a few lines down for the answer.)

The news was beginning. The station's logo appeared, the station's theme song was heard. The time had come. The image focused on an imposingly large, empty staircase. At the bottom of the stairs, on each side, there were cameras: TV cameras from the world over, feverishly waiting. There were thirty-seven of them: eighteen to the left and nineteen to the right. The image lingered a long minute on this suspenseful emptiness. The feverishness swept the cameramen. A sound was heard. At the top of the stairs appeared:

The Anchorman of the television news.

The sound of the cameras taking in his least movements to retransmit them to the other stations and, by satellite, to stations the world over while he majestically descended the marble staircase of the station's studios; the vain efforts of the reporters pushed back by the contingent of guards, trying

145

to approach him for an interview; the crackling of the non-accredited photographers' cameras, trampled underfoot by the security guards—the whole thing retransmitted to us by the invisible cameras of the Anchorman's television news station, with perfect technicality. The image vanished and we were in the studio. And the Anchorman spoke (I need not mention his name, he is a household word):

"This is ...... who is speaking to you from the studios of station ...... The top story of the day is the Anchoring of the television news that I am resuming on your station after a four-day vacation. Since six o'clock this morning, cameras from the world over have been focused on the famous marble staircase of our studios where I was due, at a prearranged time, to appear before coming here, dear viewers, to anchor your television news. For indeed..."

There could then be seen, from within the studios, the same scene as before. This time you could make out not only the anxious world cameras at the bottom of the stairs but, farther away, the anxious crowd and the station's cameras filming the images with which the news program had begun.

The Anchorman thanked the viewing audience and the other television stations and said:

"Let us now move on to the rest of the news. Princess Cordelia from San Marino has denied the reports of her remarriage with Mrs. Thatcher..."

In third place came a live interview with Tom Butler, at the Marché des Bébés Orange. This is what Carlotta was waiting for. She recorded it, then headed toward the kitchen. The meal was just about ready.

"Roast beef of angler salmon again!" she said indignantly. "Couldn't we ever have hamburgers for a change!" She cooked herself up a can of ravioli and withdrew with dignity to her room, taking her share of strawberries in cream.

Hotello followed her. As he had left unfinished his portion of mackerel, she understood that he had something important to tell her which was not for Hortense's and Laurie's ears.

* * *

With extreme silent dexterity, Hotello led Carlotta into the bathroom, while motioning, with his whiskers, that the door should be shut and the water set running to mask the sound and its origin. Then he slipped under the tub. There was the sound of a partition opening and Hotello disappeared. Carlotta, flat on her belly under the bathtub, tried following him, but despite her great agility she was not able to manage it. After a moment Hotello came back. They went down the stairs.

At the fourth floor to the left on C stairway was—you haven't forgotten—the apartment of the mysterious young man who had recently moved in. This apartment was obviously adjacent to Carlotta's and it was through the opening cut under the bathtub that Hotello was able to go out whenever he felt like it and without anyone noticing.

Hotello rang the bell. The door opened and Carlotta found herself in the presence of Prince Gormanskoï, Hortense's lover under the name of Morgan, Prince Regent of Poldevia. Hotello introduced Carlotta as her trainer for the Olympics. The Prince bowed very low:

"Delighted, Mademoiselle."

Carlotta found him nice if a bit solemn. He had, she thought, a certain resemblance to Tom Butler.

"My presence," he said to Carlotta, "my presence, Mademoiselle, is due to Love."

Carlotta became extra attentive at once. She was sure to learn a few things about Love, which would no doubt prove useful when she would meet Tom Butler in the vicinity of the Manchester studios, when she would bump into him while casually whistling a tune, in Eugénie's company (Tom Butler would be accompanied by Martenskoï).

147

"Yes, Love, Mademoiselle. I'm sure you are in a position to understand me. I love Hortense, I love her more than a little, more than a lot, more than passionately, more than insanely, and absolutely not not at all. I LOVE her." (How medieval these Poldevian princes can be, thought Carlotta, almost as bad as the Author.) "I tried to forget her when we were separated by a terrible misunderstanding. I carried out the duties of my post with an icy exactitude, but nothing allayed my distress, my infinite desire to see her again. So I decided to come back here incognito, to approach her and plead my cause, to reconquer her . . . or to die. I solicited and obtained, for this dreadfully difficult undertaking, the help of my friend Prince Alexandre Vladimirovitch, whom you know by the name of Hotello. For reasons of logistics and secrecy, he had to appear to you in a manner not quite corresponding to reality. Be so kind as to pardon him, for he did so at my request."

Carlotta pardoned.

"You no doubt haven't guessed what leads me to ask your help today." ("But of course I have a good idea what you want, old prince," thought Carlotta who wasn't born yesterday or even today for that matter. "You want to abduct Hortense with your pony Cyrandzoï and you need someone to guide him. You don't have to be a genius.")

"I'm going to tell you," the prince went on. "I saw Hortense again. Hortense loves me. I'm sure she'll accept living love's adventure with me rather than continuing on with the dull life she's leading today. With this in mind I installed, in the utmost secrecy at the bottom of the Poldevian Chapel, my personal pony, the head of the ponies of my guard, Prince Cyrandzoï."

(Carlotta pretended to be surprised and delighted.) "I know, through Hotello, of your equestrian abilities. In the name of Love, I ask for your help."

And he explained his plan to her.

Chapter 24

Hortense Chooses Adventure

After the anglered salmon, the leeks, after the mozzarella with fennel, strawberries with cream or lemon. After the white wine with cassis, the white Saint-Joseph's. Hotello was purring at his mackerel. The coffee was steaming in its dark blue cups.

Hortense and Laurie talked about marriage, love.

"Should I go?" Hortense would say with variations and circumlocutions.

"Go ahead," Laurie would answer.

Carlotta smiled inwardly. Hotello purred.

Hortense was to meet Gormanskoï. It was the Monday after Balbastre's funeral and the first time they met in Town. For they had seen each other again after that fateful Sunday. Every afternoon they took the same suburban train-steamer high speed line. They walked on the little flowers in the forest. Gormanskoï described Poldevia. Hortense painted the canvas of the great philosophical Systems. For the first time, better than during the course of the first, former love, she discovered how passion and philosophy coincide. For Gormanskoï was really listening to her. And they were not talking about shoes and dresses.

Later, as the afternoon was drawing to a close, leaving the forest, they took the train back to Sainte-Brunehilde; they got off at Bacon-les Mouillères, went to the same room at the Flaubert Hotel, and there transfigured the decor with the inexhaustible torridness of their carnal passion.

Hortense returned home, her knees wobbly.

On Monday they were to meet at the Library.

Hortense was thrown into great turmoil upon entering these august regions which had seen her love first come to birth. She had rarely come back since, because of her marriage, and also due to an inner sadness of sorts that made her avoid, without clearly knowing why, those places bearing witness to a vanished happiness. But now was another matter entirely.

Nothing, in appearance, had changed. Hortense had to ask for a book that the prince, her Lover, had brought to her attention:

Henri de Wachtendonck: *Poldevic Poldevonia*. A Natural and Cultural History of the Poldevias, both Eastern and Western. In which is treated remarkable things about these countries. Including the customs, ceremonies, laws, governments and wars of these same Poldevians.

Anvers, Christophle Plantin, 1596.

It consists of the first narrative account of a trip to Poldevia at the end of the sixteenth century, and Morgan wanted her to read it.

She handed in her request form, took out of her bag Kierkegaard's *Philosophical Fragments*, and began to read while waiting. Her heart was beating, her inner eye looking now toward the past, now toward the future. The Library seemed peaceful, as if subdued. It didn't take long to understand why.

In the battle it waged every single instant against readers who wanted to read its books, something it tolerated very badly, the Library, after long trial and error, had finally found the one unbeatable strategy: virtually definitive dissuasion. After a moment, raising her eyes from her Kierkegaard (she wasn't able to concentrate, so anxious was her anticipation of the moment she would see Him again), she noticed something: very few readers were reading; very few readers had books. Several were absently consulting dictionaries, others (those with nerves of steel) were writing letters or going through the *Newspaper*. But they had no books and none were being brought to them.

Time passed. Finally, after an hour and a half of waiting, a shiver shot through the room, for some time already crammed to bursting. Wearing an august white smock, a clerk was moving through the rows of seats with his cart, filled not as usual with books (rarely those that had been asked for but books all the same), but request forms annotated by the Library. And at once, the readers leapt up and ran every which way, into every recess of the room, forming enormous nervous lines in front of the central office. Hortense herself likewise received her own form accompanied by a salmon-colored card informing her that the requested work, because of its publication date, was not available for consultation in the reading room and that she should go to the room reserved for the exclusive use of this type of book.

It was not a room, but a rather narrow corridor in a storeroom, where ten small uncomfortable lecterns had been set up. But it wasn't the discomfort nor the dim light that was the first striking characteristic. It was that they could accommodate only one-tenth of the readers the Library directed to this sector. And it was the same everywhere. Under these conditions it had become practically impossible to consult more than one of the ten books daily that were theoretically allotted to you; for how could it be hoped, if by chance you had captured after great struggle a place in the Hemicycle, to reach in time the Reserve section or the Storeroom of faded octavos not yet sent out to be rebound. Hortense, of course, arrived too late to hope to attain her copy of Wachtendonck. But she did not admit defeat. The Library indeed possessed the second edition of the same book published by the same printer with the famous bookplate of Abraham Ortelius, and she had, through a sort of foresight (Love being her guide),

151

asked *also* for this edition. And this one was located in the microfilm room. And in the microfilm room, by unlikely chance, a place had just become free. She went over. He was there.

(We will not seek to know through what complicated diplomatic channels Prince Gormanskoï was able to assure himself [and assure Hortense, let us be quite sure] a place in the microfilm room of the Library. They were there; narratively, that is the crucial point.)

Seated side by side in front of the microfilm machine where one by one the pages of the journey to Poldevia by Henri de Wachtendonck were filing past, they whispered their love to each other. And he laid out his plan for her.

*   *   *

"Where are you coming from?"

"The Library."

"I know perfectly well that you said that you went to the Library so I would believe that you went to see your lover, whereas you went to visit your Aunt Aspasie. Why don't you admit that you had to go meet your lover?"

Let us abbreviate this painful scene.

Hortense had chosen Love's Adventure.

Wednesday evening, she made ready to leave. She got together the few dresses and shoes she would take with her for her new life. One last time she went over her apartment. The sun was setting. It was returning from Sainte-Gudule, entering her room at an angle through the large window with blue curtains. She felt a pang of anguish at the thought of the unknown life that was awaiting her, over there. Finished dressing, she stretched out on her bed with her mask, a blue domino, as planned. It was almost time. The sun was withdrawing regretfully, thinking that he would never again see Hortense in her room, a spectacle that had given him great joy. But he reflected that he would see her again once more, even better perhaps, over there. He went off happy. It was twilight.

Before leaving, Hortense recited a poem, a perfect poem because perfectly fitted with identical rhymes. "Without rhyme," as Carlotta said, "there's no poetry."

> Love love love love love love
> Love love love love love love
> Love love love love love love
> Love love love love love love
> Love love love love love love
> Love love love love love love

Love

Part Five

The Abduction

Chapter 25

The Costume Ball

The sun sat on the red horizon. Sitting did not alter its appearance, for it was round. It continued to sit until it stretched out in its bed. It turned off the light and it was night.

At first the light was pink. Next, the sky turned pale, the birds put away their instruments, their flutes, oboes, violins, viols and baroque violoncellos. There was silence. The green ray appeared over the sea, filmed by Eric Rohmer in accordance with the information provided by Jules Verne. The stars began appearing. Then things got darker and darker. It was really and truly night.

There was a full moon. It rose, casting a long sleepy gaze upon space, mystery, the abyss. We both stared at one another, it agleam, and I in pain. I was in pain because my shoes were pinching me. I was putting the final touches on my costume, my disguise for the costume ball, and the one I had picked out came with new shoes. I planned to appear in an orange Peyarot, with maroon shoes, a hemp Petticoat Lane bag, the cap of a retired employee of the Burgundian Electric Company, and a fluorescent yellow roadworker's oilskin; in other words, as I have always dreamed about dressing up in daily life, but never dared.

It was the night of the costume ball, organized by the *E Turn L* magazine, on the occasion of its thirty-seventh issue. It was the night Hortense had agreed to "elope" with Gormanskoï, her prince. He would take her away to his country. In front of the Bunker, the club where the costume ball was being held, a carriage, drawn by a pony (our old acquaintance Prince Cyrandzoï, Eugénie's and Carlotta's friend), would be waiting unnoticed. What could be more natural than a carriage drawn by a pony on the night of a costume ball?

Eugénie had told her mother that she was sleeping over at Carlotta's. Carlotta had told her mother that she was sleeping over at Eugénie's. In fact, disguised as pages, they went to the ball with Hotello (disguised as a kangaroo). At midnight, the blue domino (Hortense) and the red domino (Gormanskoï) would come out of the Bunker. Eugénie, as a page, would open the door to the carriage, then close it again once its precious cargo (the two lovers) was inside. She would climb to the co-driver's seat. The driver's would be taken by Carlotta. At a sign from the prince, the carriage would fly off along the dusty roads. At the first relay post, at the Porte Raymond-Queneau, Eugénie and Carlotta would get off, get changed, pick up their clothes and schoolbooks and, after having a good breakfast on the prince at the S + 7 café, they would go down to the métro and be off to their respective high schools. The plan had a rigorous, romantic and absolute coherence about it.

*   *   *

The silent partners of the *E Turn L* magazine had really done a great job of things. We did not drink just any old champagne, but Asti spumante, and sparkling wine from Die and Blanquette from Limoux. Root beer was served, Sprite and Mountain Dew. We ate ravioli nouvelle cuisine style, served with oysters or broccoli. Maîtres d's went around guiding kitchen boys carrying enormous cooking pots of spaghetti alle vongole. They offered some to all the masks, to all the disguises, singing:

> Spaghetti alle vongole
> What a treat for the little Astrakhole

(the accent is on the "von" in the first verse, on the "As" in the second)
and they continued:

> Spaghetti alle vongole
> What a treat for the little Angole
>
> Spaghetti alle vongole
> What a treat for the little Cinghole

After having exhausted rhymes for "gole," they moved on to *little pangolins* and even, as the night wore on, to little bunnies from Angora!

The Bunker was a former theater and the masks drifted apart in couples or small groups into the private boxes for surprise exchanges and impromptus often full of double entendrisms. Moving about among the masks, now and then I took out my notebook from my Petticoat Lane shopping bag and scribbled an observation. We novelists are always on the job. Through their costumes, I recognized P. Four., Harry M., Mat. Lin., recently come out of prison where he had been locked up by Reckless Disregard, and many others that I am sorry I cannot mention by name. I even spotted Paquerette d'Azur, dressed as Harlequin, naturally. Ph. S. had come as Cardinal Borromeo.

I passed by Père Sinouls in a wig, carrying a mug of beer, and I recognized in him the living portrait of P.D.Q. Bach, the unrecognized genius son of the great Johann Sebastian.

Carlotta and Eugénie, accompanied by Hotello-Kangaroo, did their best both to steer clear of those who fancied pages and to avoid crossing paths with Laurie, who had donned her tuxedo for the occasion and was drinking bourbon with a few friends. Through straws they sipped at their milk shakes, raspberry and strawberry respectively, while listening with their Walkmans to Dew-Pon Dew-Val (Carlotta) and Hi Hi (Eugénie). Hotello, somewhat hampered by his kangaroo costume, was lying beside them on the bar and doing his best to discourage a few mischievous or drunken masks from taking his pouch for a trashcan. Laurie's suddenly moving toward them from the other end of the bar made them uneasy. It wasn't the moment, with a mission of such importance resting on their shoulders, to get caught by a mother! So they sounded the retreat, letting Hotello seek momentary refuge under the bar, and moved along the stairs toward the august regions of the theater's balconies. They closed the doors to their box and began to read Patricia Highsmith in peace and quiet while waiting for midnight's ringing approach. For midnight was to be rung by the bell ringers Crétin Guillaume and Molinet Jean, disguised, small surprise, as bells.

The private box they had chosen was a beautiful corner compartment on the second floor of the Bunker. The curtain was down on the stage but you could sense there was a commotion behind it, producing what sounded like musical instruments. There was going to be music. The box was draped with a beautiful piece of black velour with a gold railing, and by approaching the edge you could, just barely, sneak a peek at the neighboring box. There were three Handsome Young Men involved in animated conversation. One of them was the boy from the Gudule Bar. Carlotta identified the second, who had his back toward her, as Jim Wedderburn. The third was a stranger to her. The boy from the Gudule Bar had come as a boy from the Gudule Bar and Jim Wedderburn as Jim Wedderburn. This simple fact ought to have intrigued Eugénie and Carlotta. Coming to the *E Turn L* costume ball without a mask or costume meant one of two (as a matter of fact, noncontradictory) things:

a) an insolent indifference

b) ? (up to you, reader, to fill in part b; I'm giving you a new clue, so give some thought how to use it to your advantage).

But Eugénie and Carlotta were otherwise fascinated by what the stage now revealed. It was full of instruments and musicians. The *E Turn L* magazine was offering its guests a special concert by the group Hi Hi. When Martenskoï started to sing, Eugénie clapped her hands and stomped enthusiastically in her box. Martenskoï had put on his stage costume of elegant rags and there could be distinctly seen, in flashes, amid the gyrating movements of vocal inspiration, a beautiful snail tattooed on his right buttock.

Midnight, however, was fast approaching. From two distant corners of this vastness aswarm with masks, two especially masked masks started toward each other. One was a blue domino that revealed as much as it concealed the physical characteristics of our Beautiful Heroine, the other was a red domino that did not entirely mask the princely bearing of Prince Gormanskoï. A kangaroo (under the exterior of which we are quick to point out Hotello) did his best not to lose sight of them. Finally they met up with each other. It happened almost at the top, in a calm, out-of-the-way place. They raised their masks. *Indeed it was he; indeed it was she.* Silently, without a word, they hurried toward the exit. In the street the carriage was waiting, the pony was pawing the ground, the two pages were stiffly stationed on each side of the door. The prince greeted them with a nod, and they answered him in kind, without a word. The prince opened the carriage door; Hortense got in. He followed her. The door of the berlin closed again. The pages jumped to the driver's and co-driver's seats. The prince rapped the pane, signaling as planned. The pony started moving. The berlin set off, gained speed and vanished into the night.

Chapter 26

The Abduction
followed by: Poldevians and Silicates,
A Monologue by the Author

Indeed it was she. But was it indeed he? I won't prolong the suspense any longer. It was not he! Hortense had been out-and-out abducted! And by whom? By the sinister *K'manoroïgs,* the mortal enemy of Gormanskoï and *Balbastre's murderer!* Hortense was in the hands of her lover's most mortal enemy!

But now, how had such a thing been possible?

Palpitating in her blue domino she had started out toward the red domino, as agreed, at the sixth stroke of midnight, tolled by the bell ringers disguised as Vatican bells, Crétin Guillaume and Molinet Jean. But it was not midnight! It was 11:54, and Gormanskoï, who made his entrance at the Bunker at the real 11:55 in a red domino and by a hidden stairway (always this Poldevian atavism, the oldest bandits on earth), arrived too late.

And Eugénie, you ask (don't shout, please) and Carlotta, for Christ's sake? Eugénie and Carlotta, following instructions, go out into the street to the *left* of the Bunker; they reach their posts; Cyrandzoï gives them a little signal of recognition. Hotello, blinded by his kangaroo mask at the last moment and unable to follow the blue domino all the way, carried off by a crowd of young people who had had more than their share of spumante, was not worried. He rejoined them in front of the barouche. They were waiting.

It was nine after midnight (real time). Gormanskoï appears,

looking solemn. Hortense has been abducted! The berlin which took off with her was located in the street to the *right* of the Bunker.

The pony was a Cyrandzoï lookalike; the pages were real pages in the hire of the sinister K'manoroïgs. There was even an Hotello lookalike on the roof of the berlin!

You can imagine the desolation of our quintet. Eugénie and Carlotta rushed into Laurie's arms, who was coming out of the Bunker at that very moment. They told her everything.

I said, at the beginning of the chapter, that I wasn't going to prolong the suspense any longer. I might have, indeed, dragged you along after the trusting, the all-too-trusting Hortense, on the trail of the berlin galloping through the night. I did not do so; instead, in accordance with my strict principles as a novelist, which require of me the truth and confidence in the Reader, I immediately revealed the drama. The reason is that I have in my possession a suspense infinitely more suspenseful and dramatic, whose effectiveness is dependent upon our knowing immediately what she does not yet know: that under the red domino is not her lover Prince Gormanskoï but her lover's worst enemy, and consequently hers too. And the suspense is this: is she going to discover the substitution? Yes, certainly; the resemblance is staggering, as a rabbit would say about my friends, but it's a resemblance of outer appearances, not of inner souls. It cannot maintain its illusion forever. But here's the problem: is the illusion going to last a while? In other words, not to beat around the bush for too long, as the common expression goes, is Hortense, *unsuspectingly*, going to be subjected to a fate that was considered by my predecessors to be *worse than death* (I quote)? Is she going to be saved in time? By what miracle?

We are drawn into the mazes of resemblance. For example, there is the hidden resemblance masking the intimate union of genes. Thus in *Captain Fracasse*, the Duke of Vallombroso fails to sleep with his sister, avoiding only by dramatic twists and turns, in extremis, the catastrophe of incest. In the following song, on the contrary, recognition comes too late:

> I lived with her three years
> Until the day she suddenly said
> You look like mom and dad
> Horrors! She was my twin!

Here we are confronted with a dual situation of sorts. These are Poldevian twins (for how else explain this diabolical resemblance if not by doubles, twins, even sextuplets?), the good and the evil, the white and the black, like a cloven viscount, like a modern Jekyll and Hyde, who are fighting over Hortense's precious person.

And if Hortense discovers in time that "it was not he," would it be for the better? What will she be able to do? And he, unscrupulous criminal, what will he subject her to then?

Such is the suspense, in the depths of which I leave you momentarily in order to deliver my author's monologue:

* * *

Poldevians and Silicates: monologue by the Author

We live surrounded by Poldevians. We live surrounded by Silicates, but is there, or is there not a great difference? This is the question which I would like to devote a few lines to in my introspective monologue.

Silicates, as everyone knows, form a large part of the matter composing the earth's crust. Our mother earth contains an abundant supply. We set our feet on the ground, the immemorial floor for our soles (ever since we've had feet and these feet have had soles) and we tread upon Silicates. Silica is a basic component of our terraqueous globe. Yet we were built not on a silicon but on a carbon base, as we all know. Born of the glebe, of dust, and returning to it, if the very words that the Poet places into the Earth's mouth be true:

> She knows that the Bodies she ceaselessly clasps
> Are but her Children molded from a bit of clay
> Which like regular guests go back into the house,

it is also true that we take from and give back to it for the fabric of our skeletons, chiefly carbon and not silicon. People have dreamed, and still do, about what a silicon-based life might be. But in our world, in all probability, the Silicates around us are rather inert.

The situation is quite different with Poldevians. Poldevians are everywhere. And they are alive, very much alive.

They are in Poldevia, of course, their homeland. They have been occupying since formless, indefinable times a mountainous and autochtonous region which they people with bandits and mustaches (often coexisting on the same faces). But they are also among us; in small numbers, certainly, but active. This novel I am writing, this simple chronicle of authentic events, is one proof among others. Is their influence benignant? Malignant? Should we fear the Poldevians? Are they our future, our valor, our hope? I don't know and linger on such questions.

Images flash before my eyes. Images obsess me, haunting these chapters, these paragraphs, these indented lines. I see Jim Wedderburn again, conversing with Laurie Bloom on the center bench on the Square des Grands-Edredons: a Poldevian, assuredly, at least in part. I see Stéphane again, the pastry boy, in love with the baker, Madame Groichant, the creamy and bouncy Madame Groichant. I hear it, I hear his song:

Strawberry shortcake
In Zambezia
Takes on a military tint
But in Tunisia
It's silica
That gives its clyster hue.

Tarte aux cèpes
In the station at Zagreb
Takes on a rather buttrk tint
But but in Split
It's a cooking pot
That gives its hue of grk (Poldevian wine)

Nougatine
In Indochina
Takes on an enigmatic tint
But...

—another Poldevian, a Handsome Young Poldevian Man, my intuition tells me. And once more the Poldevian/silicon link appears, in the very words of the song.

Let's take another example:

There is a lot of red hair in this novel. Laurie is a redhead, Carlotta is a redhead, Armance Sinouls is a redhead, even the female feline loved by Alexandre Vladimirovitch (who is none other than Hotello) is a "redhead."

There are Poldevians and Redheaded Females.

(Are you following me? Since I am monologuing, I run the risk of losing you along the way, so I'm checking to see if you're still there.)

There are Poldevians, Redheaded Females, and Silicates.

Furthermore, this isn't by chance. Chance isn't a narrative notion.

Silicon's electrical properties are of utmost importance. Père Sinouls wanted only silicon chips in his computer.

"They're the best," he told me.

It is not that redheaded females alone are beautiful. Hortense is beautiful. Marilyn Monroe is beautiful. I know some young beautiful brunettes; but redheaded females possess skeletons with rare qualities, electrical and otherwise.

I allow you to draw your own conclusions.

Chapter 27

Madame Yvonne; Infinity; Sinouls

Madame Yvonne had a Subject. Every woman and man who owns a bistro ought to have a Subject. There are ordinary subjects: the weather, sports, taxes, TV, the weather, TV, . . . They form the bulk of bistro-talk, outside of the technical exchanges about orders and the phone. But there is also the Subject, which lends the café its color, its texture, its originality. The topic can be, and most often is, one of the ordinary topics; but in that case the café is an ordinary café. They have their place. It can be a burning subject like Poldevians, Red-headed Women, Silicates. In those sorts of bistros the Real Problems are brought up, set out. There is talk about legislation, morality, dangers, about trains to rectify the real problems once posed. Now I stay clear of those sorts of bistros. There are more and more of them, which is too bad. As Père Sinouls says: "Shitting on the sidewalk is no way to pose the real problem of clean streets."

But there are cafés with original Subjects, around which a certain network of regular clientele comes into being, those who know that they can come in for a drink but also to bring up the Subject.

Madame Yvonne's Subject was Infinity. She was indebted to Père Sinouls who had opened in front of her one of the most imposing, even frightening infinities, that of cosmic spaces, with their galaxies like grains of sand, with their colossal arms of spiral nebulas, and the efforts (oh how very slow) of light to transform it into a warm living community, a bistro of worlds in effect. It gave her a fright but fascinated her at the same time. As the song goes:

> When I was little
> My teacher told me
> The sun's far away, the stars even more
> Between it's cold and dark
> Every night it empties out
> Now at the thought I can't sleep any more

> *Refrain:*
> Laplace, Le Verrier
> Kepler and Ptolemy
> Tycho Tycho Tycho Tycho Brahe
> Galileo Copernicus
> Galaxies and Kubrick
> Quasars, pulsars, it all makes me gobble aspirin.

She made it her Subject.

Little by little, she had discovered, through Père Sinouls or other customers, that there were loads of other infinities. Aristotle and Cantor often came up for discussion. She never lost her weakness for geometric infinity, or for celestial spheres, but on occasion she did not turn up her nose at Numbers, or Time.

Thus she had problems with her Gudule Bar waiters. Either they weren't interested in Infinity, didn't understand a thing about it and didn't give a damn; or else they were all too interested and held the irreducible finitude of orders in contempt: 1 Perrier, 3 Oranginas, 2 glasses of beer, 6 coffees, 4 Suzes, 5 Fernet Brancas—what possible importance could these have when there were highly inaccessible cardinal numbers at your disposal? Why not bring 5 Perriers, 1 Orangina, 4 glasses of beer, 3 coffees, 6 Suzes, 2 Fernet Brancas? It never amounts to more than a sadly finite permutation of beverages. The customers were rarely in a position to understand this point of view.

She lost her employees rather quickly. Cautious, she interviewed them *beforehand* on the Subject, and hired them only if their answers appeared satisfactory. But that wasn't sufficient. When the one we call the new waiter at the Gudule Bar, a Handsome Young Man, showed up, she started up the conversation without much hope. She received a shock. The young man had some very precise ideas about Infinity. He didn't believe in it: "10 to the 23rd power," he said to her, "did you ever go see it for yourself?" Madame Yvonne thought she'd choke with indignation. But at the same time, good bistro owner that she was, she saw the full advantage she could draw from the situation. Certainly it wasn't the first time she'd heard the reality of Infinity denied. But in general it was with arguments that were soft, "screw-it-allish," as Père Sinouls put it. But now this young man held some very clear ideas, some highly technical reasonings that gave her (even though she did not understand them) hope. She immediately took him into her service. She saw she had every reason to be pleased. He did his table-waiting well, which she had anticipated since she took him for a stolid finitist (something he wasn't), but in addition he brought to the Subject the shock of renewal that injected a second youth into the discussions of the regular clientele.

* * *

It was the day after the abduction of Hortense, the news of which had spread through the neighborhood like lightning, giving rise to the craziest speculations and a wave of concentrated fury. Hortense was loved. "Not stuck-up," "always a kind word to say," "pretty as a picture" could be heard. Madame Groichant practically went into mourning. All hopes were placed in Blognard. This very fellow passed by, looking preoccupied. The two cases were connected. More tears were shed on Balbastre. People trembled even more.

But that didn't get in the way of the Subject. Events pass away, but the Subject remains.

Present there was (I mention only the mainsprings of the discussion, not stray remarks from among the chorus of occasional customers):

— Madame Yvonne and the waiter from the Gudule Bar
— Retired Admiral Nelson Edouard
— Père Sinouls
— Professor Girardzoï
— Hotello.

Père Sinouls and Professor Girardzoï had come in together. They were leaving the Center for Comparative Patanalysis. Professor Girardzoï was the author of the Sublime Language (LAPEFALL) which Père Sinouls used in his computer; the language where there could be no bugs, those little harmful creatures that gobble up programs; yet where there seemed to be one all the same and of quite some size. (Turn back to chapter 17.) "I don't understand," Sinouls would say, "don't sit there and tell me that Gödel's theorem is not valid in Poldevia." (LAPEFALL is Poldevian, as is its inventor, Professor Girardzoï.) It was said in jest. But the professor did not laugh. He ran his hand perplexedly through his beard and murmured. "Perhaps we ought not to tickle the Divinity's toes too much." Père Sinouls had gotten thirsty and suggested continuing with something to drink.

Madame Yvonne had just started the ball rolling:

"He," she said to Admiral Nelson Edouard while pointing to the Gudule Bar waiter, "does not believe in Infinity. He thinks that everything is finite," she added unwisely.

"I did not say that," the boy started up, "I said that your notion of infinity is vague and confused, as is the one about finitude, coincidentally. I said," he went on, preferring to address the admiral (it already was an old controversy , between the two), "that you, like the near-totality of admirals and mathematicians for that matter, don't even know what a number is. And your notion of a 'Great Number,' for example, comes from a pun on the word 'number' in which you confuse counting little strokes with arithmetical calculations. Let's take 65536, for example. It's a way of writing a number that both you and I can count. But then you tell me there's a number that you call 2 to the power of 65536, that is 2 multiplied by 2 multiplied by 2, 65536 times, and that this number exists because you would be perfectly able to count up to it by lining up little strokes. But my answer to you is: how do you know? Let's suppose that you're able to draw your little strokes very quickly, let's say the very short time it takes light to cross the diameter of a proton; let's also suppose that the age of this portion of the universe in which we wet our feet is somewhere around twenty billion years old; you will need, using your own ways of designating your numbers, 19684 to the power of 10 ages of the universe, that is a 'number' that is written I followed by 19684 zeros, to reach the one you name 2 to the power of 65536. And I will not follow you. You remind me of the teller who was given a stack of one hundred dollar bills. He had to check that there were a thousand. He began counting, 1 bill, 2 bills, 3, 4, . . . he counted up to 73, then stopped. Because it was working up to 73, it would surely work up to a thousand."

Admiral Nelson Edouard objected that all that was very fine and dandy but somewhere there was a big pile of all the whole numbers, that there was an infinity of them, everybody knew that, all you had to do was draw up a few examples, and that he would continue to believe in the real and actual infinity of the ensemble of all whole numbers, as he had been taught by senior ranking Admiral Dieudonné.

"Once again," the waiter from the Gudule Bar went on, "I'm perfectly content for you to believe in all the infinities that amuse you, but I would like you to make an effort to be a little more specific about what you mean by that."

He drank a small bottle of Vichy water to get a second wind.

"Whole numbers get worn out," Professor Girardzoï whispered cryptically with dreamy strokes to his beard.

The waiter from the Gudule Bar continued as follows:

"Let's take another example: a sheet of regular typing paper where you can type, let's say, 1500 characters. These characters are chosen from the keyboard available on your machine, let's say, 80 characters. For you, Admiral, there are 1500 to the power of 80 different texts that you can type on your machine. You type" (he was addressing Madame Yvonne now) "a first character, chosen among 80 available to you. Then a second, quite independently of the first. That already comes to 80, multiplied by 80 more possibilities. Each time that you type a new character, you again multiply by 80 the number of text-beginnings thus produced, each one different, correct?" (Madame Yvonne uttered an "oh" of surprise before the enormous bulk of the different typewritten pages fluttering down in front of her. It was worse than a spaceship.) "But for me," said the waiter, "I don't even know if the 'number' of texts is finite. Perhaps it's infinite. Perhaps the ensemble of all these texts cannot be considered in a sound manner. Perhaps it will always be possible, in eternity, to type a new page, different from the others. Infinity is not so far distant in space, in time and in thought. Perhaps it's by giving ourselves over to the most banal activities, picking the petals off of a daisy, a little, a lot, passionately, madly . . . serving 2 Perrier, 5 Oranginas, 6 glasses of beer, 1 coffee, 3 Suzes and 4 Fernet Brancas that we plunge into Infinity."

The Admiral said nothing. He was a little shaken and was thinking about writing a letter to NASA to counsel caution.

Père Sinouls took advantage of the lull to launch on lambda-calculus. The gathering broke up.

Chapter 28

Balbastre's Secret

And the victim? Has he been forgotten? After the sorrow, after the pity, the indignation, is the time for forgetfulness already here?

Not for Blognard, in any case. He takes out of his bag a 100 percent goat's milk yogurt: "This natural yogurt is obtained from goat's milk delivered each morning to the Cheese Company of Bacon-les-Mouillères by the shepherds. To savor all its delicacy it can be eaten plain or with sugar. On the other hand, it can also be complemented very well with jams, or an aged liquor. Professor Shahaniskofï has demonstrated that yogurt . . ." Blognard read these lines on the yogurt's cardboard wrapping which he has just removed. The "on the other hand" of the fifth line preoccupies him a moment while he dips his spoon into the white creamy surface inside the dodecagonal container.

He's in his office, Quay of Entry-into-the-Matter. It's dawn of the sinister day following Hortense's abduction. The sun is not proud; it feels vaguely responsible. Blognard carried the yogurt and the file for the Case in a plastic bag his wife gave him. It's one Madame Blognard ordered from Laurie's catalogue. It comes from The Hound of the Baskervilles Bookstore on Baker Street in London. The name appears above the portrait of a dog made of the same characters.

Blognard has not forgotten Balbastre. He has been seen these past several days in the Square des Grands-Edredons on all fours, not because he is trying to put himself in the victim's skin in order to think like him, as he usually does (something he has more or less given up doing, at least in such form), but because he is seeking to retrace the dog's last steps, to reconstruct his last moments. All the streets surrounding Sainte-Gudule had been examined with a fine-tooth comb; Arapède went around to all the houses and gathered testimonies in his large notebook. There was one of major importance.

Blognard ponders this a long while, from time to time casting a penetrating glance upon the photos of Balbastre that he placed on the desk next to the yogurt container.

Madame Anylline, the dry cleaner from Rue des Grands-Edredons, moved out of number 53 Rue des Citoyens, D stairway, second floor, following a nasty fright (see "The Dry Cleaner Wrangler," one of Blognard's investigations, in the same collection), and had taken refuge at her daughter's, Rue des Milleguiettes, opposite the Sinouls house. She is very sensitive to noise, and sleeps little. The night of the crime, with her elbows leaning on the window ledge, she saw Balbastre. No doubt she also saw the criminal but from behind. She describes him very precisely as being of medium height, and having no special markings. Blognard has no hope of getting very far with this description, other than that the criminal was a man, but even that was not absolutely certain. In Madame Anylline's eyes, ever since The Case of the Dry Cleaner Wrangler, all criminals are men and all men, criminals. What is infinitely more important is what she said about Balbastre's behavior: "He went up to him wagging his tail, the poor dear. He looked so happy! And then all of a sudden he stopped, sniffed, and took off running as if he had the devil on his tail. And it was really true, he did have the devil on his tail. The other took off after him. Arrest him, Inspector, I beg you. He's certainly the same person as mine" (the criminal called the "Dry Cleaner Wrangler" had been unmasked but not arrested).

Therefore: *the victim knew his murderer.*

Or rather, this meant one of two things was true:

— the victim knew the murderer; he's a friend (the wagging tail), he goes up to him. But he makes an unexpected gesture, a threatening one. The victim runs away, he follows him, catches up to him before he reaches the sanctuary of Sainte-Gudule, strikes. First scenario: very probable;

— or else, the victim *thought* he knew the murderer. The victim moves toward him, with the same reactions of joy as in the first scenario. Spots his error (at night, resemblance need not be very great), draws back, runs away, with the same result as in the preceding case. Second scenario: possible.

In the first scenario, there is something in the victim's life that placed him into relation with the murderer.

In the second scenario, there is someone in the victim's life who resembles the criminal. He is the one that must, first off, be sought.

The two scenarios presuppose the same initial searches. But afterward, in the second case, if the murderer is a perfect stranger, and the resemblance deceptive and coincidental, Blognard will not have made much progress.

Yet Blognard does not think so. There is an axiom in criminal matters valid for a civilized country such as ours. *One murders only people one knows.* It's not like in America. Over here we have the feel for human relationships. The first scenario does not benefit, by this axiom, from any additional light. In the second, on the other hand, the result is that Balbastre knew X. *The murderer knew X* (leading to the weak form of the axiom that Blognard, in accordance with his method, states as follows: *One is murdered only by someone one knows, or else by someone who knows someone one knows*).

In either case, Madame Anylline's testimony is of major importance and indicates the course to follow. Blognard finishes his yogurt (a 3.5 ounce container).

There is a *secret in Balbastre's life.* It is going to be revealed immediately (time is running out, we are nearing the end). Arapède is the one who brings it. He comes into the office with the Poldevian inspector. The Poldevian inspector is not feeling quite himself today. He is walking on eggshells, with infinite precaution. Perhaps he has gout, like Sinouls. He sits at the edge of his chair and listens attentively. And watches. As do we.

Arapède places a VCR on the desk, plugs it in and inserts a cassette. On the screen they see appear the *Handsome Young Man from the jeans commercial.* He advances along the beach, he looks at the sea. The female bathers lean up on an elbow to get a glimpse of him when he slowly takes off his jeans and has nothing on but his bathing suit, while standing opposite the sea. Then he turns around, facing the silhouette running toward him along the blue salty ocean. He holds his jeans in his hand, they see the brand name. They see, clearly, the snail tattooed on his left buttock. Most especially they see the end of the commercial. The dog leaps upon him, kisses him effusively, makes off with the jeans which he drags along the sand, taking great care to leave the brand name visible.

The dog is Balbastre!

Some while before the beginning of the events that make up our story, Balbastre read in the *Newspaper* a piece of information that greatly upset him: a Machiavellian individual had perfected a gadget that prevented dogs from barking. Yes, from barking. An anti-barking collar was slipped around their necks and presto, an anti-barking frequency was emitted, penetrating the skull of the unfortunate creature and inhibiting the barking hormones. He remained silent. He wanted to bark, he opened his mouth, and he could not! The tests had been conclusive; they were moving on to mass production. Balbastre was crushed. He talked it over with a few dogs; they all agreed on one point: action had to be taken, and quickly; otherwise, what had already happened to smokers was going to happen to dogs. Act they must, but how?

First of all, by a campaign to raise public awareness: creating a lobby made up of dogs, their owners, little girls or boys who had dogs or wished to have them. To do this, a Law of 1901 Association permit was a must. Therefore Balbastre created the SPB (Society for the Preservation of Barking). But for the SPB to thrive and be effective, money was necessary. For a long time Balbastre sought financial backing for the SPB. Membership dues, though substantial from the start, were not sufficient (the sum had been fixed at the equivalent of one bone a month, which, with the progress of Green Europe and the elimination of compensatory sums, did not allow for much of anything, not even enough to pay for a one-minute commercial spot on TV).

But it was precisely this idea for an SPB commercial spot which gave Balbastre the solution to his financial problem.

There existed, in the canine community, individuals whose resources surpassed the rather modest means of the mass of members. These were the dogs who worked in advertising, those who served as models in the sequences lauding products for dogs, or for little girls and boys (it always makes a nice impression to have a dog around when selling cookies or detergent). This represented enormous potential resources. And that's why, duty-bound as president of the SPB to set an example, Balbastre decided to do something he had always shunned, out of purity of conviction: to take roles in ads.

At the agency responsible for the film, Arapède had dug up test clips and rushes. Balbastre could be seen with the Handsome Young Man of the commercial. They were obviously on the best terms. They were great buddies, said the head of the agency. They didn't leave each other's sight.

At last, a lead.

(Let us reassure the Reader. Despite Balbastre's death and the resulting decline of the SPB, brought about by clashing strategies in the heart of the Office, the terrible threat that dogs are facing is for the moment averted: the anti-barking frequency product is not really perfected. Rather extensive tests brought to light undesirable *side effects*: barking, certainly, disappeared. But the test animals began biting, biting compulsively, frequently, silently [and for a very good reason] and without warning.)

Chapter 29

The Dew-Pon Dew-Val Concert

The unspeakable premeditated act of Hortense's abduction hastens the end. At midnight, in front of the Bunker, we are practically less than twenty-four hours away from the final act.

It is twelve after midnight in front of the Bunker. Gormanskoï is there, Cyrandzoï the pony, Hotello, Carlotta and Eugénie, and Laurie who joined them. There is no joy sparkling in their eyes. All thoughts are on the impending dangers that hang over Hortense.

And now?

By enthusiastically accepting to help Hortense and the Prince (an enthusiasm aroused by the prospect of driving a barouche drawn by her friend Cyrandzoï), Carlotta had not, in the first second following the "yes" she had given to Gormanskoï, reflected on the implications of the time and day chosen for the operation. The second after, she did think about them, and she felt a moment's hesitation. But this hesitation was not visible (except to the trained eyes of Gormanskoï, Hotello, Eugénie [who in addition knew] and Cyrandzoï). This date, this hour were terrible blows for Carlotta. On the same date, at one in the morning, the first major night concert by Dew-Pon Dew-Val was being held in the City, in the large hall of the Nadir, a glass cheese cover able to hold an audience of ten thousand. Thanks to the Author, who had stood in line for seats (something they couldn't do because of their classes), they were sure of getting in (and that's the reason they had each announced they'd be spending the night at the other's since the concert would end at an extremely latish hour). Carlotta *had to give up the concert.* She staggered under the blow, but inwardly. Not a single facial muscle quivered, not a single one of her red hairs trembled. Her voice remained steady when asking the prince for instructions.

But now Hortense's abduction meant it was still possible, by acting quickly, to get to the concert in time. Prince Gormanskoï, despite his distress, did not hesitate. "Mesdemoiselles," he said, "my barouche is at your disposal." And while Laurie went to have a drink with the prince to keep his spirits up, the barouche, drawn by Cyrandzoï, at a breakneck speed conducted Carlotta, Eugénie and Hotello toward the doors of the Nadir.

There were ten thousand seats, but thirteen thousand tickets had been sold, not including the counterfeits. Since the seats were first come first served, and since classes were over, the expectant audience had been waiting for the doors to open. Carlotta and Eugénie would have done likewise, but now their only hope was to get seats somewhere in the last rows. That was without figuring on Hotello, who was more and more regaining his real look, that of Prince Alexandre Vladimirovitch. Displaying his diplomatic safe-conduct pass at the stage door, he got them into the hall, and they found themselves in the very first rows. Cyrandzoï, a secret admirer of Dew-Pon Dew-Val, would also have liked to go in. But Alexandre Vladimirovitch pointed out to him that while he, as a cat, could pass more or less undetected in this crowd, the case would not be the same for a pony. And what's more, the barouche needed to be guarded, since it would be taking them back to Square des Grands-Edredons after the concert. Cyrandzoï sighed but understood the soundness of the arguments.

We will not go into the hall of the Nadir. It doesn't suit our age. At any rate, we will find out what happened from the

firsthand account that we took down from Carlotta herself,
who called us as soon as she got in the door and had taken a
bath to calm down.

* * *

It was wild   yes   it was wild   really wild
I can't go into it
I was wild too
It's no big deal   don't get the doctor
Well you got an idea what the square is sizewise   well they
had planned on ten thousand
there must have been twelve thousand of us in there moving
around
Hi   OK fine don't get him
You know
And all screaming their heads off like crazy
And not just the girls   the guys too I can't go into it
I sat on the right
On the right if you know I mean
To look at Tom
You get me
I was hysterical   hi-ster-i-cal
OK the wall, made out of papier-mâché
The lights right in our faces the lights really wake you up
There was this lady she had this umbrella
Maybe for stars falling out of the sky   and spiked heels
right on my feet
I turn around I see Aurélia   no first off I *hear* Aurélia
It was easy who else but her could hit those high notes I was
sure
she doesn't even recognize me
that concert was a real horror show it was from hell
Carlotta was wild
he comes on   he gives us a *big* smile   there's somebody

else   he gives her a *big* smile   I could've killed her
Aurélia shouts   where is she   let me at her
she looks at Tom through her binoculars
Tom noticed me   I'm sure Tom noticed me
galloping brain pneumonia   not me no way
it's not possible   I can't go into it don't get the doctor   I'm
the one that wild girl   yes, that's right   cramped neck
Tom in front   lit by a red spotlight   in a T-shirt
he's up there   he's a little tall in front on stage just a little
      I can't go into it being in the first row with Eugénie and
Aurélia
screaming their heads off in there
screaming   clapping their hands
I don't even have feet anymore
they come on
there's this one girl trying to climb up on stage she gets
thrown out
us three we're the craziest of the bunch
but that's not me! that's not Carlotta! no Carlotta's wild
Joseph*
Joseph goes "you're the best . . . audience"
Joseph takes off his jacket he's got on a red T-shirt with stars
great special effects   we scream for him to turn around
in the first row they're all fainting left and right
there're just girls in the first row
I'm busting out of my jeans
Tom says "Good night! . . ." we yell, "Oh NO!"
They come back
They sang: ...... and then ...... and then ......
Fine OK
We get home I put on the radio   what are they playing

---

*He was the third Dew-Pon Dew-Val: there's Tom Butler, Tim
Butler (no relationship), Joseph Le Just; and the musicians.
(*Author's Note.*)

Dew-Pon Dew-Val   I can't go on

Such was the Dew-Pon Dew-Val concert in the Nadir hall the night Hortense was abducted.

Chapter 30

The Exhumation

Despite her unwavering attention and intense participation in the concert, Carlotta had noticed, to the left of the stage, Inspector Arapède. Since the little she knew about him did not indicate he was an enlightened fan of Dew-Pon Dew-Valian music, she was surprised. She observed that his eyes remained riveted on Tom Butler. You didn't have to draw her a picture; she was quite capable of adding up two and two and getting four, and even of adding two to two thirty-seven times, taking away one and getting the right answer. This inspection was not at all to her liking. And her uneasiness turned into alarm when, going backstage, Hotello again in the lead with his safe-conduct pass, and then to the barouche to tell poor Cyrandzoï all about the concert, Carlotta heard the inspector say to one of the guards: "Please be so kind as to deliver this summons from Inspector Blognard to Mr. Tom Butler. At ten o'clock this morning he must be at Père Sinouls's. The address is on the summons." After having gone home to take a bath, discussing it with Eugénie and phoning the Author, she made the momentous decision to *cut her morning classes*, especially her geography class dedicated to New Oil Producers: (II) Poldevia.

She would go on over to Père Sinouls's.

What was going to happen there?

For several years it has been known that a healthy reaction to the excesses of the modern world has brought on a renewed interest in certain things and methods of the past, unfortunately over-neglected in obeisance to the god Science, an idol with clay feet: cancer is treated with chamomile tea, politicians consult fortune-tellers and crystal balls before making a decision; faced with the obvious dangers and harmful effects of anesthetics, certain hospitals have even decided to perform operations for appendicitis without putting patients to sleep, or not operating on them at all. In short, minds are fortunately in the process of evolving in every field.

The search for legal evidence has not escaped this great movement issuing from the depths of our society. The great medieval traditions have been rediscovered. Blognard could not remain insensible to the pressures from above to take some account of these discoveries, or recent rediscoveries, in his investigations. Despite his reluctance, and Arapède's blatant skepticism, he had decided to try out one of these methods, one of history's most famous. In fact, to be quite frank, he expected nothing directly from the method itself; but he did not object to subjecting certain suspects (he was beginning to have very precise suspicions) to this proof, one so extraordinary to modern people that their reaction could well prove interesting.

Indeed, it was clear that the Poldevian connection had been confirmed and made highly explicit ever since the discovery of Balbastre's connection with the Handsome Young Man of the commercial and Madame Anylline's testimony. All those Handsome Young Men who looked alike and had recently popped up in the neighborhood were going to have some explaining to do. It was possible, perhaps, to save some time by means of the rather Gothic experiment that was going to be attempted. And saving time was important, for every hour that passed increased the danger for Hortense, whose abduction Blognard (without knowing everything we do) was convinced was the work of the same culprit. He had therefore summoned Tom Butler, Stéphane, Madame Groichant's new pastry boy, Molinet Jean and Crétin Guillaume; Jim Wedderburn could not be found. The Young Man from the commercial had not yet been identified. Feeling a little more like himself and a bit nervous, Inspector She. Hol., contrary to his habits, accompanied Arapède and Blognard. Père Sinouls, forewarned and ironic, was awaiting them on his threshold, Pilsen in hand.

Everyone entered. They went to the garden.

* * *

Blognard wanted to examine (it was a sort of examination) only one suspect, only one "alleged Poldevian," so that his reactions would be both pure and unambiguous. Therefore around Balbastre's open grave there were only the inspectors, Père Sinouls and myself (we were no longer suspects, nor could we be suspected in the least of being Handsome Young Men!). Carlotta was also there, but concealed by the poppies. The suspects were grouped in the Sinouls living room, under the portraits of Balbastre, and awaited their turn. To calm his jitters, the pastry boy, Stéphane, was singing a verse of his love song, the one that had gotten him two good slaps from Madame Groichant:

> When I'm close to your cream puff
> I feel all quadrumanous
> Light your little oven
> I'll bring the propane
>
> *Refrain:*
> Make no mistake, you're aiming
> Straight for my poor heart's filling.

Tom Butler drew near. He was still in his stage clothes and was shivering, despite the climbing temperature on this radiant morning.

They were going to be subjected to the Proof by Confrontation. In this Proof by Confrontation, from the Middle Ages, the suspect is placed in the presence of the victim's cadaver. If the victim reacts, that is if his wounds begin to bleed again, or if he gives any other sign of this sort, then the suspect is guilty. Total confidence is placed in the victim; the reasoning is that he will not lie.

Therefore, under the magistrate's order, they had proceeded to exhume Balbastre. There he was, intact (embalmed, which gave him a certain similarity to the Emperor Nero), unchanged, at rest in his glass coffin.

"Come closer!" said Blognard to Tom Butler.

And the three inspectors drew near also, all the better to watch the victim's reactions. Tom Butler took a few steps to the edge of the grave. Carlotta came and stood just behind the flowering jujube.

Balbastre's fur bristled, that is, stood up like Madame Mac Miche's on her head in *A Good Little Devil* by the Comtesse de Ségur, née Rostopchin.

It was a *sign*. Blognard took a step forward. Tom Butler went pale.

"Wait!" shouted Carlotta, rushing between Blognard and Tom Butler. She was using her body as a sort of rampart. "Wait, you're forgetting the Counter-Proof."

"That's true," said Blognard, "that's true, Mademoiselle Carlotta, we're about to forget the Counter-Proof. What do you suggest?"

Without hesitation, Carlotta told him. They waited. Everybody stepped away from the grave, and Balbastre's fur, subdued, fell back down. Policemen arrived, carrying a VCR, set up within range of the coffin. Carlotta inserted the cassette she had asked for, and on the screen appeared the singer from the group Hi Hi: Eugénie's Love of Her Life, Martenskoï. With Tom Butler remaining at a certain distance, everybody drew near Balbastre.

Balbastre's fur, once again, stood on end.

"You see," said Carlotta, triumphant, "your Confrontation proves nothing."

"Perhaps," said Blognard. "My thanks, Mademoiselle."

Despite the joy caused by her victory, which had saved, so she thought, Tom Butler from being immediately arrested, Carlotta returned home feeling that, despite everything, he was still under suspicion. For the experiment suggested a number of conflicting conclusions, not all of which would clear Tom Butler (which ones wouldn't?).

Her troubles were not over. She must, she must . . .

She must find and free Hortense and thus discover the real culprit.

Part Six

Carlotta versus K'manoroïgs

Chapter 31

Blognard

After Carlotta's intervention and departure, Blognard appeared disconcerted for an instant. It seemed to me he had intended to arrest Tom Butler, or at least to hold him for questioning. But clearly he had changed his mind. He announced that the Proof by Confrontation was temporarily interrupted and Balbastre was lowered back into his grave. His fur had gone down after all the commotion, whose interpretation was so elusive.

After leaving the garden the three inspectors headed for the Gudule Bar. Madame Yvonne, presently deprived of her new waiter who numbered among the suspects in the Poldevian sphere of influence, was serving the customers herself. She came up to us, with a hint of coldness, though she liked Inspector Blognard, one of her regulars, who had brought her customers by making her café into his headquarters during The Case of the Hardware Store Horror. But she was certain of her employee's innocence; he had such extremely interesting ideas about Infinity! She would have been deeply sorry to see him go off to prison. Of course, if he had really murdered Balbastre ... But she was sure it just wasn't so.

She brought the inspector his usual lemonade (two squeezed lemons) flavored with grenadine syrup; and a Canada Dry for Arapède. One day the latter had cast doubt on an interlocking assemblage of Blognard's proofs (he was, lest we forget, skeptical by nature, education and philosophic resolution) by saying: "Those aren't proofs, even though they seem to be, they're Canada Dry proofs." He had been rather proud of his comparison and had taken to drinking Canada Drys (or Canadas Dry, I'm not sure).

Madame Yvonne set her tray down on the table and said:

"And for the Handsome Young Man, what will it be?"

Inspector She. Hol. looked surprised at this manner of address. He remained silent a long while, still a bit uncomfortable in his chair, then answered:

"My name is Shorulikeszaky Holamesidjudji. I am honorantissimentibly, Madame Yvonne, honorextreme..."

In short, he wanted a Fernet Branca. He took just a sip and then in one gulp threw down Count Branca's wild liquor without batting an eyelash.

His contribution to the investigation up to that point had been nil. He stuck to Blognard and Arapède like glue, listened attentively, took copious notes, read all the dispatches, admired Blognard's techniques and equipment, especially the computer terminal, but he came up with no opinion aside from comments on the customs of the City's inhabitants as compared to those of the Poldevians in the Capital.

Since his oral interventions were nearly interminable, Blognard was not in fact angry about not having to discuss the She. Hol.-ian hypotheses, which would have taken up a lot of time. At the start he had asked the Big Boss how long he was going to be obliged to put up with the inspector's being around, but the answer given him was that it would only be to the end of the investigation, that it was insisted on in high places, and that all he needed to do was unravel the enigma as quickly as possible if he wanted to be rid of him. Blognard, bearing his pain patiently, showed him the greatest courtesy, indeed showed him everything. He didn't listen, so to speak, to his words; Arapède simply continued to translate them into a more succinct French, to which he answered in monosyllables.

The trio of inspectors in the shadowy café did not notice

Hotello, curled into a ball on a chair, observing them between his half-closed lids. He had stopped dyeing his fur (the dissimulation was no longer necessary around Laurie and Carlotta) and Alexandre Vladimirovitch's natural coloring, his princely gray-black with a hint of blue, was reappearing here and there.

"Arapède," Blognard suddenly said, "could you go over to the office to see if I'm there, I need to think."

"Yes, boss, I'm off."

"Oh, since you'll be passing it, can you ask the Cipher Office if they've decoded the telegram sent yesterday by the Poldevian Bureau of Investigation? I'd like finally to have an answer to my questions."

"OK, boss," said Arapède.

He headed toward the café door and Inspector She. Hol., after a few seconds' hesitation, followed him. Alexandre Vladimirovitch unwound himself along the top of the chair and then under the table, leaving in turn.

Blognard remained alone.

*   *   *

After the pro-Butlerian coup de theatre staged by Carlotta, he wasn't as confused as he seemed to let on (and we too, for our part, almost allowed ourselves to be taken in).

After Arapède, She. Hol. and Alexandre Vladimirovitch (whom he had spotted, since the latter did not seek to conceal himself from the inspector's eyes) left, his attitude changed, at first imperceptibly, then more and more perceptibly. First he finished his lemonade with grenadine, then took a pack of Callard and Bowser's English liquorice from his pocket, opened it, pulled out and unfolded from their black and silver wrapping two pieces that he stuck simultaneously into his mouth and began to chew dreamily. His eyes sought Madame Yvonne.

"Another?" she said.

"The same thing," Blognard answered.

And this interchange in the Gudule Bar echoed at the very heart of the Case, transposing onto the linguistic level of bistro conversation the philosophical, metaphysical, onto-logical, rhythmic and now detective paradox of the *same* and the *other*.

Madame Yvonne brought over a second lemonade with grenadine.

Blognard was beginning to have an almost perfectly clear idea of the Solution. All that he was missing, unfortunately, was the crucial evidence. He slipped on his glasses, took from his attaché case a folder containing a considerable number of typed pages and avidly poured over them. For a long while there could be heard only the sound of liquorice chewing and the crumpling of papers that had a tendency to stick to enliquoriced fingers. Finally he stopped his reading, looked at Sainte-Gudule, drank, set his glass down.

Suddenly he slapped his forehead with his palm: "But that's it! How stupid of me!" he exclaimed.

"That's it!" he repeated with obvious satisfaction.

He had found the answer.

(And you?)

Warning: we have not said that the last piece of the puzzle had just found the place Blognard had been vainly seeking in his dreams for several chapters. Puzzles are the scourge of detective novels. Never, Blognard thought while furiously tossing down a new detective novel he had allowed himself to get caught up reading, never does a mystery's solution turn up like a missing piece of a puzzle. If the author gives us a jigsaw, it's because he doesn't know his craft.

So we are forewarned.

Chapter 32

Where Is Hortense?

This is precisely the question Hortense was asking herself as we rejoin her: "Where am I?"

Let us leap back to that fatal midnight when the berlin stationed in the darkness swallows her up and carries her off.

There was a whole series of surprises, of small disappointments.

For starters, she really would have liked to have been able to give Carlotta and Eugénie a kiss of thanks. She understood the urgency, the imperious necessity of putting as many as possible Poldevian leagues between herself and any potential pursuers before dawn, but this meant leaving the City, perhaps for a very long while; she wasn't going to see Carlotta again very soon. She got a little lump in her throat. She would have liked to kiss her, tell her to kiss Laurie, also that she would write, that she would be in touch, that she wouldn't forget them. She was somewhat disappointed.

Then she found Morgan strangely silent.

She continued to call him Morgan inwardly as in the old days: "Prince" struck her as too cold, too solemn, too ceremonious. "Prince Gormanskoï" made her burst out laughing. She said it only with a laugh, only when playing lovingly with him, in the bedroom at the Flaubert Hotel, in Bacon-les-Mouillères. Throwing herself with a sigh of joy on the black velvet cushions of the barouche (she thought she had understood they would be red), she whispered, "Oh, Morgan ..."

"What?" he said, as though he didn't understand his own name.

She thought he was agitated.

But she was just a little bit surprised. Normally he showed an imperturbable sangfroid. And his eloquence was great, especially in moments of intimacy. Tonight he said nothing; and if his hands proved loquacious, it was with a violence, an awkwardness that she found unfamiliar. He is truly disturbed, she thought.

The barouche came to a stop. As he got out, "Morgan" (we are placing quotation marks to indicate that we should not forget we are dealing with the false Morgan, the terrible K'manoroïgs) took a blindfold out of his pocket and muttered something about "security." She let herself be guided along, a bit puzzled. She thought they were supposed to leave the City as quickly as possible. There had been a hitch, she was told, the plans were changed; they would stay in a hiding place for a few days, while waiting for the "coast to clear."

Blindfolded she climbed a stairway, guided, once again awkwardly, by "Morgan"; she stumbled on one or two steps and she heard him expressing impatience. She didn't like that.

Entering the room, she made out something like a horse smell. The room was large. The furnishings were at a bare minimum: a bed, a sink, a chair. On the bed, cushions. On the ceiling, a large mirror reflecting the bed. The colors were violent, the silk sheets, salmon pink. She had the fleeting impression she was in a brothel (a literary brothel, naturally, in line with the descriptions furnished her by the very best authors). She was surprised, yet again surprised. There really had to be an emergency for this weird room to be the only possible place. "Morgan" closed the door. Alone at last.

* * *

What distinguishes the Same from the Other, good from evil, black from white, when the exteriors are identical, the surfaces similar, the twilight gray? How to grasp, beneath an apparent identity, the contrary abysses within? Without realizing it, this was the problem facing Hortense. And every passing minute this problem became more urgent. Totally unawares, she herself attempted to hasten the fatal outcome.

Hortense leaped on the bed where "Morgan" joined her with the same enthusiasm. She wanted, as quickly as possible, to seal carnally (what a choice expression) their permanent (at last!) union, and to erase even in memory her mistake, the mistake of their separation. And he was as much in a hurry; a little too much perhaps. His state of commotion was considerable but, contrary to all their habits, past and present, he seemed to want to dispense with the long kisses and caresses which for Hortense made up a concerted part of their mutual turmoil. She let herself be undressed while laughing, and once naked she wanted to return the favor. But he refused and removed his own clothes. It was then that a first alarm of sorts went off inside her, but she paid it no mind. Naked as well, in all his strength (he was a Handsome Young Man), he joined her. It was the ultimate moment, soon to become intimate. And our one thought is: Hortense is lost!

No!

She said to him: "What's this, are you forgetting our agreement?"

And indeed he was forgetting it, for the very good reason that he didn't know it. Since he wanted her deceived, absolutely deceived, therefore consenting (there would be time later to undeceive her and to conduct events in *his* less degenerate manner), he moved aside (observe how our inevitable description of the movements in progress is perfectly decent) and Hortense, turning him over on his stomach, leaned over to kiss him on his left buttock, in the spot where the sacred snail, Trademark of the Poldevian Princes, was located.

It was their invariable lovers' ritual and it was impossible for their union to be consummated without it.

She leaned over and,
abruptly,
in a flash,
in a lightning flash, she saw again,
an indelible image,
her dream of page 100.

There was the snail, there were the groups of diacritical dots, but,
they were not in the right place.
Instead of

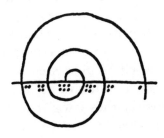

6: Gormanskoï

it was

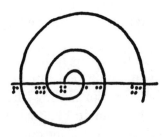

3: K'manoroïgs

It was not Morgan, but K'manoroïgs. She had fallen into the hands of the enemy.

What to do?

She had three seconds to think up something.

Suddenly tossing herself backward, she said with a laugh, "Now catch me!" She pretended to run away. K'manoroïgs could take no more. He threw himself upon her, seeking, without too much violence all the same, to achieve his ends by transforming a certain leg-angle, which Hortense still laughing had brought back to zero, into another, more favorable to his designs, the closest possible to his preferred angle, 2π over 3 (expressed in radians). Right at that moment, with the utmost naturalness and playfulness, and the utmost unintentionality in the world, Hortense let him have a good shot with her knee.

Where? you say, a shot with her knee where?

Where I think.

During the three seconds that were hers, she had eliminated the other conceivable solution, a migraine, since she was dealing with an unscrupulous criminal. A knee-shot was her only resort. It was a magnificent shot, worthy of the Lézignan rugby team on one of their best days. It must be said that Hortense was worked up more with fury than anxiety about her fate. That helped.

K'manoroïgs let out a yell. Hortense overflowed with entreaties and distress, but she had nothing to fear for the rest of the night. It would take him at least twelve hours to recover.

Chapter 33

I: The Captive   II: Deliverance

I: The Captive

When she awoke she was alone. She inspected her surroundings. It took no time at all. The room was padded, noises from the outside (vague bell sounds) reached her faintly. There was only one lamp. She had no idea where she was, nor how much time she had at her disposal to do something; not much, no doubt. Whether he had suspicions or not concerning the unintentional nature of the miraculous knee-shot, K'manoroïgs, once recovered, would be anxious to do only one thing, complete the work he had undertaken the day before, and what could she do then to oppose it? He wouldn't hesitate in the least to resort to violence, of that she was sure.

The door opened and her jailers entered. There were two of them, two Handsome Young Men, perfect duplicates of each other. Without a word, without speaking to her, they placed on the chair a tray containing a glass of orange juice and another of passion-fruit juice; a pot of coffee; a pitcher of real cream; a teapot; a plate with six pieces of toast, two croissants, one brioche; two eggs with bacon, and Cambridge sausages; two small jars of jam; butter; sugar; a black paper napkin. Hortense thought: force-feeding geese; but nevertheless she ate with gusto.

At the same time as Hortense's two silent guards came in, there also entered a bat. The men seemed to know it and paid it no mind. The bat fluttered close to the tray and asked permission to drink a little milk. Hortense agreed very gladly.

And so it was that she learned from the bat, who was named Batwoman, that she was imprisoned in the belfry of Sainte-Gudule!

When Batwoman understood that Hortense was being held in this place against her will (at first the bat had thought it was a clandestine tryst), she was highly indignant and immediately offered her services. Hortense eagerly accepted. Taking a green pen out of her bag, she wrote a message on the paper napkin for Hotello, which she then entrusted to Batwoman, who placed it at once in her scarf.

Molinet Jean and Crétin Guillaume came back into the room (for K'manoroïgs's accomplices were none other than they) to get the breakfast tray. Still without a word, they went out, turning the key twice in the lock, again without paying any mind to Batwoman who left with them.

Hortense lay down on the bed and waited.

To pass the time she read a little Spinoza.

* * *

II: Deliverance

After spending two hours fluttering fruitlessly around the square, knocking on windowpanes with no success in awakening Laurie, Batwoman intercepted Alexandre Vladimirovitch at the moment he was coming out of the Gudule Bar. It was almost eleven o'clock in the morning. Matters were urgent.

Alexandre Vladimirovitch woke up Carlotta who, after defending Tom Butler, had fallen asleep on her bed still dressed. She rushed to the bottom of D stairway. Just then, along Rue de l'Abbé-Migne, Stéphane, Madame Groichant's pastry boy, was arriving with a tray of cream puffs on his head that he was going to deliver to the Gudule Bar. Alexandre Vladimirovitch and Carlotta looked at each other. A delay, and it would be a disaster; a mistake, likewise disaster.

"Let's go," Alexandre Vladimirovitch mutely muttered with his whiskers.

"Let's go," Carlotta answered mutely with her red hair topped by a beautiful white straw hat with a black band. The hands of Sainte-Gudule's were drawing near eleven o'clock. Stopping Stéphane at the fence of the square, Carlotta explained the situation to him. Stéphane understood in a flash. Standing in plain sight at the foot of the belfry he started to sing at the top of his lungs the first verse of his song, "The Linzer Torte":

> Linzer torte
> In the Dead Sea
> Takes on a caramel tint
> But in Alsace . . .

He could not go any farther. Coming out onto the balcony of their apartment in the belfry, Molinet Jean and Crétin Guillaume, unable to stand such horrible words and melody (not to mention the voice), began shouting vulgar insults in Poldevian. Stéphane dished it back.

But meanwhile, climbing the northern face of the belfry along a rope ladder hooked to the gables by Batwoman, Alexandre Vladimirovitch slipped through the back into the room deserted by the bell ringers. While Carlotta was laying hold of the keys to the prison where Hortense was shut up, Alexandre Vladimirovitch leaped onto the bellpull which he began to peal madly. At once the bell-ringing accomplices of the criminal charged up the stairs leading to the bell room to thrash Alexandre Vladimirovitch who, abandoning the bells with one prodigious leap, landed on the chestnut tree so as to get back down to the square.

However, as he was setting foot on the ground, Molinet Jean and Crétin Guillaume, who had raced down the stairs four at a time upon seeing him leap, loomed above him. And now on the other side in the direction of Rue des Mille-guiettes his retreat was cut off by the murderer himself! The latter, in fact, had been at the end of Rue des Grands-Edredons and was about to turn into Rue Neuve-du-Presbytère when the bells tolled by Alexandre Vladimirovitch told him that something serious (for him) was in the works around Sainte-Gudule's. He rushed toward the square, knocked Stéphane over into the basket of cream puffs, and now the three bandits were closing in, their eyes wild with malice, toward the apparently defenseless cat at the foot of the chestnut tree.

It was at that moment that the training given to Hotello by Carlotta produced its most spectacular results. In three leaps, shtack, shtack, shtack, Alexandre Vladimirovitch jumped above Molinet Jean, Crétin Guillaume and then the fence on the square and lithely landed on the running board of the barouche drawn by Cyrandzoï, driven by Carlotta, and inside of which, safe and sound, was Hortense. Carlotta and Cyrandzoï negotiated a sharp turn with a controlled skid onto Rue de l'Abbé-Migne, and all the three criminals could do was gaze helplessly at the back of the carriage driving away into the distance down Rue des Citoyens.

The whole thing had lasted six minutes and sixty-one typewritten lines, one of the shortest and most spectacular escapes in the history of the adventure novel.

Chapter 34

An Interview;
and other considerations

The denouement is fast approaching. You can sense it by various clues, not the least of which is the relatively few number of pages left to be read.

Hortense is safe, we suppose. She escaped both the median and perpendicular virulence of the enemy, Prince K'manoroïgs, Balbastre's murderer. We would like all the same to be quite sure that he is no longer in a position to cause any harm and is put behind bars. To do so requires knowing under what identity he has been hiding until now. He was unable to leave the City. The Porte Raymond-Queneau is closed off by the police. Hortense herself was not able to leave and is at this moment at Laurie's.

Here's what we still need to do before winding up the four six-paragraph chapters left us: provide the *explanation* given by Blognard, where the criminal's alias is revealed, backed by evidence; and in which, more generally, all the necessary loose ends are tied up. In addition, there is the *epilogue*, to bid farewell. We'd previously planned on an *interview*, and a *stew*.

But there is also the *acknowledgments* and the *table of contents*. They are also generally found *within the book*, though outside of the story strictly speaking. That appears legitimate regarding the contents; but as far as the acknowledgments go, I am in total disagreement.

Let me explain. After your novel has appeared, the people you know can be divided into two categories: those who are in it, disguised in one way or another, and those who are not. Those in the novel are either happy or not about the way they are portrayed, but as far as that goes there is nothing you can nor wish to do. That's how you wrote your book, you put them in it, you can discuss it, offer explanations. On the other hand, it is far more difficult to explain yourself to those whom you have *not* put in the novel. You meet X (or Y) and he/she says to you: "And here I thought I was your friend and you didn't even put me in your novel." To avoid these reproaches, a very common tactic consists of putting all your friends, relatives and acquaintances in the acknowledgments, at the beginning of the book. In such a way you can answer: but I put you in the book, didn't you see the acknowledgments? This sounds like a dodge, a joke in bad taste on the meaning of "being in the book." Nobody's satisfied. Therefore I decided to place the acknowledgments *within the text,* and I do so at this point, now that we are reassured about Hortense's fate, and before the developments of the utmost importance that are going to recapture our attention. So then:

ACKNOWLEDGMENTS

I thank my Publisher, and all his Publications, without whom and which this book would not have seen the light of day.

I thank my relatives, my friends and acquaintances. Without them, if they had not been what they are, that is, my relatives, my friends and acquaintances, respectively, I would not be what I am and consequently this book would not have been written.

I thank my characters, whose warm support allowed me to see this project through to a successful conclusion.

There remain three special thanks:

a) to Père Sinouls, who was so kind as to pass on to me the contents of the sign located at the entry to the forest;

b) to Monsieur Pierre Lartigue, for reasons that will become apparent in the next chapter;

c) to Mademoiselle ....e ...e, to whom I addressed the following letter:

> Dear ....e,
>
> There is in this book, as you have been able to note when reading the typed manuscript, a character by the name of Carlotta, whose story and adventures present certain similarities with your own.
>
> I know, as you told me, that the first name Carlotta is the one you'd give anything in the world to have.
>
> I hope you will excuse me for having used it, thus showing, by its very use, that despite the similarities, it is not about you but about a mere young lady of paper, who has but two dimensions, one shadow.
>
> My very best wishes,
>
> The Author

I add here, for completeness' sake, the traditional warning: Responsibility for any coincidental similarity with living persons is accepted; any express similarity will be most vigorously denied.

*　*　*

Before withdrawing from the book (a decision I made with regret, but which I made all the same) there remains one last intervention.

I made an appointment to see the criminal. I knew not only his identity, that of Prince K'manoroïgs, but I also knew his alias. He agreed to see me only after reading the note I had transmitted to him, which left no doubt about the fact that I knew.

This step was extremely difficult for me. My every instinct urged me not to negotiate (I was going to negotiate, I confess) with the brutish murderer of my friend Balbastre, whose death had plunged a whole family into a state of affliction. But I was aware of my duty; I could not shirk it.

I will not reproduce his words, I will not do him the honor of allowing him to speak in this chapter. I will simply report what I told him.

I told him it was best not to be stubborn, to recognize his defeat. What's more, if Blognard hadn't already discovered the truth, he'd not have been long in finding it out. At any rate, despite the horrible nature of his crime, he would not be risking very much. Given his princely status and the complex relations that our country maintains with Poldevia (oil interests, among others), he would be merely deported. Let him then go and continue his vendetta in his own country and leave ours, its dogs and young women, in peace. Such was my advice.

But mind you, it was only advice.

I knew perfectly well that he thought he had one last ace up his sleeve and that, without any further hope of realizing his ignoble objectives regarding, on the one hand, the principality, and on the other, beautiful Hortense, he could nevertheless continue to do harm. How? By means of a scandal: revealing the real reason Prince Gormanskoï was present in the City, the activities he engaged in in order to live here for several months without any outside contact, with no resources other than those he could obtain through work. Once the details were worked out, this is what he wanted to throw to ravenous reporters, creating enormous diplomatic difficulties and perhaps in a small way saving face among his supporters for the shame of his failure.

And nothing (his venomous grin betraying that such was his belief) could prevent him from taking such revenge because of his defeat.

Nothing, really?

And that was the moment I laid my cards on the table.

If ever he opened his mouth to spread such slime, here is what I would do. Little by little I would leak out, until it reached Poldevia, the story of how Hortense had escaped him, had escaped the fate he had in store for her, how she had tricked him and rendered him impotent. Then we'd see what his supporters would think about that. And I had evidence: the very film of the scene that he had planned very differently and which he wanted to revel in at his leisure (having set up for this purpose a hidden camera in the belfry room where he had shut up Hortense).

The poor wretch's haughtiness vanished. He was vanquished.

Chapter 35

Stew

Life goes on. The sun sets, rises, sets, rises, sets, rises, sets, rises, sets, rises. The weather is nice.

For Père Sinouls, it is the dawn of a stew day. Despite his sorrow, he doesn't feel too poorly. His program is running: Blognard and he each found their diskettes that the criminal had switched around. His big toe hurts him less, thanks to a miracle drug. He sings in his bath:

> Colchimax in your bones
> Drips down, down,
> Colchimax in your bones
> And your gout is gone.

First he goes to Rue du Pre-Tout-Pres to buy some tea for Madame Sinouls at Fiançailles Soeurs (when leaving the Sinoulses' you turn *right* on Rue des Milleguiettes, you turn right at the end of the street, and it's the first on the left). The august house of Fiançailles Soeurs has been recently modernized; brunch is served. A Handsome Young Man weighs out his tea for him. "Oh no," thinks Sinouls, "enough Poldevians!"

Back home, Sinouls speeds his daughters off to the market. It's a stew day.

In the Sinouls dining room, along with the family, are also seated Arapède, the Blognards, the Reader (who is filling in for the Author, tactfully absent from the end of the novel);

above them, the portraits of Balbastre commissioned in homage by Père Sinouls, the painters and their spouses: the Getzlers, then, and the Guyomards. Finally, Monsieur Pierre Lartigue, chef, collector of *sextines* (a rare variety of mushrooms). Madame Getzler, Madame Blognard, and Monsieur Pierre Lartigue are dedicated stew makers, and the day's stew was prepared following a special recipe compiled by Monsieur Pierre Lartigue, who gave the Author the authorization to reproduce it, for which he was thanked in the preceding chapter. There is one more guest: the waiter from the Gudule Bar. He is being watched. He remains impassive.

Monsieur Lartigue rises and reads while eyeing the tureen opposite:

For six persons, four pounds of meat,
Beef: half rump, half chuck, several rinds
Of pork *ventrêche*, fresh belly, a calf's foot
Olive oil, onion, two liters of wine,
A carrot, a clove of garlic, orange peel,
Salt and pepper, bay leaf, and a sprig of thyme.

Place at the bottom of an earthenware jar the thyme,
The carrot sliced in rounds, the bay leaf, the meat
In large cubes. Salt and pepper. The orange peel
Is placed on top, with a little oil. (Rinds,
Ventrêche, belly are cold.) Cover with wine.
Seven or eight hours in the cellar. You're at "the foot

Of the stairs." Carefully slice the calf's foot
In half and open it. Bay leaf and thyme
Float on the marinade. Draw off the wine
And be sure to drain well the cubes of meat.
Belly and *ventrêche* are diced up. The rinds
In strips. They are as tough as a peel,

Fatty yet supple, under the knife's blade. Strange
    peel!
In a cast iron cooking pot, scorch the beef. (The foot
Is set aside.) And brown the onion. Then put in the
    rinds,
The *ventrêche*. The heated marinade (thyme,
Pepper, and fresh carrot) is poured over the meat.
Submerge a nice clove in the fragrant wine.

(If need be, add a little heated wine
Over everything.) In the black pot the orange peel,
Warmed nicely, from now on suffuses the meat
With its aroma. For five or six hours the foot
Will cook down with the garlic clove and thyme.
Immerse the *ventrêche*, belly, and rinds.

Never will they seem as tender, these rinds.
In an earthenware jar, next add the wine
With these cubes done to a turn. (Remove the
    thyme!)
Draw over the top like a beautiful ribbon the orange
    peel.
Let cool. The jelly from the calf's foot
Will congeal, brilliantly, around the meat.

   Meat that is eaten cold accompanied with rinds,
with juicy foot, all the flavors intermingled! Oh the
wine, the garlic jelly and the orange peel, the thyme.

Everybody's salivating impatiently.
Time to eat!

Chapter 36

The Explanation

Inspector Blognard addressed his audience.

The scene was the Sinouls garden. Following tradition, he had brought together all the witnesses, all the suspects, the press (Monsieur Mornacier, present without his wife Hortense, who was recovering from her nasty fright over at Aunt Aspasie's in Sainte-Brunehilde-les-Forêts), the Reader. So Hortense was missing, the Author, as was Carlotta, who had to record the greatest hits of Dew-Pon Dew-Val for a girlfriend. Tom Butler was there. There was also, of course, Madame Yvonne, Madame Eusèbe, Madame Groichant and Madame Anylline. In short, just about everybody.

The victim was also there, in his glass coffin, a palpable regret for all in attendance except for three, a standing reproach to the criminal and his accomplices. Officers maintained a discreet watch from the rosebushes.

Inspector Blognard, I said, addressed his audience.

"In this case, there never existed any doubt about the identity, in the final analysis, of the criminal. All of us knew, from the start, that we were dealing with Prince K'manoroïgs, one of the six Poldevian princes. My apologies for recalling things everyone is familiar with, but it's necessary for my exposition. Prince K'manoroïgs, we know, anxious to become First Prince Regent in place of the First Prince Regent, Prince Gormanskoï, whom I greet (he is among us, as is the murderer, but incognito), Prince K'manoroïgs devised a diabolical plan. It was while setting this plan into action that he was led

214

to murder the unfortunate victim, loved by all, Balbastre. (Alexandre Vladimirovitch uttered a few reservations, with his whiskers.)

"Gormanskoï and K'manoroïgs are not the only princes involved. There are six of them. They all look astonishingly alike, as one of Captain Jonathan's pelicans resembles another pelican from a Far Eastern island. Each is a Handsome Young Man. All six have a genius for disguise. And they each have a *sacred snail* birth- and trademark tattooed on their left buttock, as you can see for yourself, on your diagram (see page 136). Please look at them carefully. The difficulty is apparent. To determine which one we are dealing with is no easy matter in everyday life. Their internal differences, certainly, are enormous. One, Prince Gormanskoï, is perfectly good; the other, Prince K'manoroïgs, perfectly evil; the others are more like us, with some good and some evil in equal measure.

"Now, we are faced with nine possible suspects, among whom should be found the two princes, and in particular the criminal we are searching for, so we can render him harmless. These suspects, all Handsome Young Men with a Poldevian connection that is either flaunted or revealed, here present, are:

"1) the new waiter at the Gudule Bar; 2) Tom Butler, singer of the group Dew-Pon Dew-Val; 3) Inspector Sheralockiszyku Holamesidjudjy; 4) Jim Wedderburn, Laurie's colleague; 5) Stéphane, Madame Groichant's pastry boy; 6) the young man from the commercial, Balbastre's friend; 7-8) Molinet Jean and Crétin Guillaume; 9) Martenskoï, the singer of the group Hi Hi.

"But let us proceed in order."

The inspector broke off. Escorted by Arapède, all the suspects went out of the garden and entered the house. Inspector Blognard took a swallow of his grenadine lemonade and calmly broke the wrapper of a pack of Callard and Bowser's liquorice. He went on:

"When the suspects return, the truth will make itself known. You have all the clues in your hands. You should know who is the criminal, and who Prince Gormanskoï. This invitation to draw conclusions is traditional in the classic detective novel and the Author insisted that I extend it to you. It is done."

There was a silence. Alexandre Vladimirovitch knew but could say nothing. Carlotta had understood everything but was not there. The others didn't give a damn. The Reader, maybe?

"No volunteers?" said Blognard. And he shouted: "Arapède, it's time, they can come back." And he added for the public's benefit: "The suspects more or less voluntarily went along with my little demonstration."

All heads turned toward the platform which had been set up in the garden behind Balbastre's grave.

The suspects returned.

*   *   *

They had changed clothes. Now they were wearing only bathing suits. There was an "oh" of amazement. Stripped of their disguises and garments they were indeed absolutely identical, absolutely interchangeable. Anyway, six of them were. The three others, when the eye grew accustomed, could be distinguished by small physical disparities. There existed, indisputably, two groups of suspects.

They all stood up very straight, very calmly, facing the audience. "Thank you, gentlemen," said Blognard. "Let us proceed in order, and by the process of elimination. It is clear, and I see that you yourselves have noticed it, that three of these gentlemen ought to be, right from the outset, eliminated. Namely, numbers 7-8 and 9 from our list."

Molinet Jean, indeed, and Crétin Guillaume resemble Poldevian princes, pass for Poldevian princes, but are not

216

Poldevian princes. They are accomplices of the criminal, they had a hand in the murder by pealing the thirty-three strokes of midnight that terrorized the victim. They had a hand in the abduction of Hortense by sequestering her in the half-belfry of Sainte-Gudule's to satisfy K'manoroïgs's ignoble fancy. Fortunately, thanks to the courage of our Beautiful Heroine, and to the sangfroid of our friend Batwoman, the abduction failed.

"Turn around," he said to the two bell ringers. On their left buttock appeared two sacred snails. "The essentials are roughly there, the Trademark exists. But these snails are imitations, crude imitations. There isn't even the right number of dots, not to mention their order. And in addition . . ."

As he spoke he had gone up to the platform, flask in hand. He poured a little liquid on a piece of cotton that Arapède handed him, rubbed, and *the snails disappeared.* Molinet Jean and Crétin Guillaume were led off; and then there were seven.

"Let us move on to Martenskoï," said Blognard. "Martenskoï, although perfectly innocent of the crimes, is also not one of the six princes. He is the Prince's cousin, thus he has a sacred snail, but" (Martenskoï turned around) *"on the right buttock."*

Martenskoï went off in turn. And then there were six.

"I am not going," said Blognard, "to ask these gentlemen to turn around also. That's where the Solution lies, but that's not how we ought to arrive at it, how I myself arrived at the truth. The Truth issues from an act of reasoning, as faultless as possible."

The princes also withdrew and returned, once again in their disguises.

"To arrive at the Solution," said Blognard, "what does a detective do? He reflects, he interrogates, he notes, he

217

guesses, he remembers, he scrutinizes, he does everything a detective should to solve the mystery. I could have, obviously, proceeded likewise. But I ask you, how do we know everything the detective does and discovers, everything important to know, the victim's secrets, the criminal's schemes, etc., etc.?"

How indeed?

"The answer is quite obvious. We know *by reading the novel.* Everything necessary, and nothing but what is necessary, is found there. We have no access to anything else, at any time. 'We' meaning detectives, victims, criminals, minor characters, heroes, heroines and the Reader.

"As soon as I discovered this, the path to follow was very clear. I asked the Author for the typed manuscript of the first thirty-five chapters (that's what I was reading in the Gudule Bar in chapter 3). Let me say in passing that the manuscript is loaded with typos: the Author's typewriter has an unfortunate tendency to transpose letters in words and this tendency becomes more and more unpleasant as you move through the text. Let me also take advantage of this opportunity to point out, following a phone call from Madame Getzler [confirmed by my wife, Madame Blognard] that there is a serious mistake in the stew recipe such as Monsieur Lartigue gives it. It calls for *cansalade,* and not *ventrèche*).

"I read and that's where I put my finger on the Solution. Let's review from the beginning the problem facing the criminal. He is a prince but he wants to become First Prince, Prince Regent rather. The order of Poldevian precedence is in fact as follows: the Regent Prince, as you see on the Trademarks page, has number 6. But, by doing this he is going to disrupt the order of all the princes. And this disruption will occur according to the immutable and traditional order instituted by Arnaud Danieldzoï in the eighteenth century. Number 1 comes in the second place; number 2 in the fourth; number 3 in the sixth, the most important; 4 comes in the fifth; 5 in the third; and 6 in the first, as follows:

$$1 \ 2 \ 3 \ 4 \ 5 \ 6$$
$$6 \ 1 \ 5 \ 2 \ 4 \ 3.$$

"But mind you, what I'm telling you now is merely a confirmation! We can just as easily find what interests us, the names of the (disguised) criminal and Prince Gormanskoï's, simply by reading our text with attention. In what manner? I am going to make a comparison."

"What, huh, what's that you're going to make?" asked Père Sinouls, suddenly awakened by an elbow-jab from his daughter Julie on his left and his daughter Armance on his right, for he had fallen asleep and was snoring.

"I am going to make," repeated Blognard, "a comparison. When we read the novel we are, in our capacity as readers, like someone watching the movie *Lady in the Lake*, adapted from the Chandler novel. In that movie, directed by and starring Robert Montgomery (Chandler himself wrote the screenplay and followed the filming), the camera was permanently positioned to give the impression that what you saw was seen through the eyes of the hero, Marlowe. This is exactly what happens in the novel. Author and Reader, we are eyes that see and we see what is said that we see. Now, during the course of the novel we meet, by *seeing* them, the six Poldevian princes one after the other, *in a certain order*, which is the one I pointed out to you at the beginning of my *exposition*. Let me recall it (I retain only the six in question, I eliminate the false and extraneous princes):

"1) the new waiter at the Gudule Bar; 2) Tom Butler; 3) Inspector She. Hol.; 4) Jim Wedderburn; 5) Stéphane; 6) the Young Man from the commercial.

"Next, and as the novel progresses, we meet them again. But *not in the same order*. In which order? As you have guessed, in the order precisely imposed on every princely permutation, the one displayed a bit earlier:

6 1 5 2 4 3.

"But that's not all; the princes continue appearing; and they continue turning, in a cosmic spiraloid cosmogonic and snailesque ballet, they turn according to the same movement, so that they then appear in the series:

3 6 4 1 2 5.

Then in the series:

5 3 2 6 1 4.

and so on. They appear *six times each*.

"How does that help us to find *who* Gormanskoï is, who K'manoroïgs? It's very simple.

"When we see Prince Gormanskoï with our own eyes for the first and only time, in what series position does he appear? *In that of the Young Man in the commercial.* Prince Gormanskoï *is* the young man in the commercial, who was Balbastre's friend (and this was an additional reason for the murderer to strike with the brutality familiar to us).

"And the murderer? How to choose him between the five others?

"The murderer is exposed because he *appears seven times.* This supernumerary, disorderly, immoderate, arrogant appearance betrays him. And he's *number 3:* Inspector, or rather the false Inspector Sheralockiszyku Holamesidjudjy!

"He is the number 3 who wants to become number 6. What's more he is so obsessed by this desire that he can't manage to say correctly his assumed name; he shifts syllables each time he pronounces it, and I'll let you discover how!"

Blognard triumphantly scanned the audience which let go an "oof!" of relief. K'manoroïgs was brought back, in handcuffs (made of Poldevian gold in accordance with the bilateral treaties). On the chairs there were scattered movements, preliminary to leaving.

"One last point," said Blognard, "it won't be long before I'll have solved the last mystery, which concerns the victim.

"It wasn't to get Gormanskoï accused of the murder that K'manoroïgs struck. Such an eventuality was absurd. And for us to ascribe this motive to the criminal, all we have is the testimony of the criminal himself, suspect at the very least. The real motive is the following: he wanted to make off with the manual of the new programming language invented by Professor Girardzoï, LAPEFALL, Language to Put an End Finally to All Languages. With this language in his possession, once he became Prince Regent of Poldevia, he would be able to satisfy his demented dreams of power. However, to get his hands on the manual, one copy of which was at Père Sinouls's, take it and photocopy it, Balbastre had to be eliminated since he would rather have been killed than to allow this theft."

"Oh, my poor old pal!" said Sinouls, moved.

Epilogue

Chapter 37

A Farewell Ceremony

A few days had gone by, and a sober and moving ceremony was taking place in the Sinouls garden. Hortense and Prince Gormanskoï had come to place flowers on Balbastre's grave before their imminent departure for Poldevia: a bouquet of thirty-seven black tulips, the most beautiful kind.

The weather was still beautiful but cooler and Hortense was in a light exclusive (I mean to the exclusion of other materials) dress, requested by her lover Morgan in memory of their first meeting. In the spring sunshine, which did not obscure one single feature, she looked even younger and more beautiful than usual, and Père Sinouls, who was following the scene good-naturedly, also remembered the first time he had glimpsed her, in Rue des Citoyens, in a similar dress. There are still many more really great moments in this world for an old voyeur, he thought.

Hortense and the prince were leaving the next morning, in the barouche, with Cyrandzoï, driven by Carlotta. They would go as far as the Porte Raymond-Queneau, where they would have lunch near the tollgate, in our day converted into a Customs station for entering or leaving the City. There, they would take leave of Carlotta, Alexandre Vladimirovitch and Cyrandzoï, who would return to Square des Grands-Edredons to continue on with their training for the hurdles race, with a view to the Olympics. Alexandre Vladimirovitch was unable to make up his mind whether to leave Laurie and Carlotta, his two redheads. Who would blame him?

Hortense was daydreaming in the soft sunlight. She kissed Père Sinouls, went out onto Rue des Milleguiettes and gradually disappeared from your sight.

But *you* stay right where you are.

Excerpts from the secret notebooks of the Author making their exclusive world premiere to English-speaking readers at the Translator's insistence

May 26, 1988. Received a letter from the Publisher; the success of *Hortense Is Abducted* is such (already more than 2,200 returns out of 2,300 delivered to bookstores; Finnish translation virtually assured) that he is urging me to send him the sequel, my promised third volume: *Hortense in Exile.*

Sent off the synopsis at once, very original I believe: the novel will recount twenty-four hours in Hortense's life in Poldevia: going out one morning to the capital city's supermarket located in the palace of her lover Prince Gormanskoï, she loses her way and begins a period of wandering for a whole day long during which many adventures come her way. The FANTASTIC IDEA is the following: each of the chapters will be the very precise transposition of a canto from a verse epic by an ancient Greek poet I've discovered, a certain Homer. The *Odyssey* is what his work's called. Hortense will be the hero Ulysses, Gormanskoï, the hero's wife, Penelope, etc.

June 4. My publisher is raising all sorts of objections, half of which I don't even understand. I don't think he grasps the mythical and **allegorical** dimension of the project. Plus the hyper-hard porno slant of certain episodes (like Hortense-Ulysses' emerging from a lake stark naked and appearing before Chinese launderers on the beach), far from damaging the book's reception would make seizures at customs a certainty, not to mention trials, maybe even demonstrations by the Silent Majority and a sermon by Monsignor Fustiger, which from the publicity point of view would be quite effective. The parallel Ulysses-Hortense is worth at the very least a good hundred Ph.D. dissertations and incorporation into the syllabi of all sections of Feminist Studies Departments (it does not seem to be known that the *Odyssey* was written by a woman! I have this piece of information from a certain Samuel Butler). This will reinforce my image as an uncompromising, unjustly neglected postmodern author. The literary world will finally realize that *I am an essentially private man whose insensitivity to the judgments of public opinion deserves to be universally recognized.*

June 18. Nothing to be done; he persists in not understanding. Ought I to address myself directly to readers, to the public? Launch an appeal over the airwaves?

August 4. The matter's settled. This very night I've given up the idea. In fact, I've got another, even better one. Let me jot down the synopsis right away, so I won't forget it:

—having arrived in Poldevia with the man who is now her fiancé, Prince Gormanskoï, Hortense grapples with the intrigues of the Court, assembled in the château of Lsnrkaï. She suddenly notices there's something rotten in the Kingdom. During the Prince's absence, power was usurped by the Prince's own mother, and his stepfather (whom Gormanskoï suspects of having hastened the end of his father's life). Hortense, with the help of a pastor, a certain Yorickskoï, urges him to take action, but he hesitates. In a *gnomonologue* (a literary genre I hope to launch on this occasion) of great philosophic, poetic, and esoteric depth which I've just begun ("to be the being or the non-being, all the while being beingness or non-beingness, that is the tormenting question," etcetera), he questions himself before passing into action. His enemies meanwhile urge him to abandon Hortense and conspire against the heroine's life, whom they plan to eliminate by having her catch pneumonia (by means of prolonged submersion in a bathtub); fortunately Laurie and Carlotta save her in the nick of time, while Gormanskoï is dying, apparently, in a duel (*apparently*, only because he too must be saved for the other volumes in the series).

September 11. My publisher has returned from vacation. He sent me back the synopsis, angrily crossed out in red ink and deleted every which way, plus in the margin: "See Sh—!" Cycling really doesn't agree with him. I don't understand what he means, but my guess is that he's not at all pleased.

September 12. One catastrophe brings on another. A letter from Laurie arrived this morning, messing up my whole plan:

> You lose a few marbles, or what? You think we'd go off and bury ourselves for six months in Poldevia to get that airhead Hortense out of where she's gone and got herself in a jam all over again? Speaking for myself, I'd go for a week at the max, all expenses paid. But don't count on Carlotta. This summer she's starting work on her Ph.D. in Boogie-boarding on the San Diego campus.

Betrayed by my characters, denied my publisher's support, misunderstood, abandoned, lost, short of inspiration, having mislaid my electric bill that I should have paid the day before yesterday at the very latest, what am I going to do?

Jacques Roubaud

PIERRE ALBERT-BIROT, *Grabinoulor.*
YUZ ALESHKOVSKY, *Kangaroo.*
FELIPE ALFAU, *Chromos.*
   Locos.
   Sentimental Songs.
ALAN ANSEN,
   Contact Highs: Selected Poems 1957-1987.
DJUNA BARNES, *Ladies Almanack.*
   Ryder.
JOHN BARTH, *LETTERS.*
   Sabbatical.
AUGUSTO ROA BASTOS, *I the Supreme.*
ANDREI BITOV, *Pushkin House.*
ROGER BOYLAN, *Killoyle.*
CHRISTINE BROOKE-ROSE, *Amalgamemnon.*
GERALD BURNS, *Shorter Poems.*
GABRIELLE BURTON, *Heartbreak Hotel.*
MICHEL BUTOR,
   Portrait of the Artist as a Young Ape.
JULIETA CAMPOS,
   The Fear of Losing Eurydice.
ANNE CARSON, *Eros the Bittersweet.*
LOUIS-FERDINAND CÉLINE, *Castle to Castle.*
   London Bridge.
   North.
   Rigadoon.
HUGO CHARTERIS, *The Tide Is Right.*
JEROME CHARYN, *The Tar Baby.*
MARC CHOLODENKO, *Mordechai Schamz.*
EMILY HOLMES COLEMAN,
   The Shutter of Snow.
ROBERT COOVER, *A Night at the Movies.*
STANLEY CRAWFORD,
   Some Instructions to My Wife.
RENÉ CREVEL, *Putting My Foot in It.*
RALPH CUSACK, *Cadenza.*
SUSAN DAITCH, *Storytown.*
PETER DIMOCK,
   A Short Rhetoric for Leaving the Family.
COLEMAN DOWELL, *The Houses of Children.*
   Island People.
   Too Much Flesh and Jabez.
RIKKI DUCORNET, *The Complete Butcher's Tales.*
   The Fountains of Neptune.
   The Jade Cabinet.
   Phosphor in Dreamland.
   The Stain.
WILLIAM EASTLAKE, *Castle Keep.*
   Lyric of the Circle Heart.
STANLEY ELKIN, *Boswell: A Modern Comedy.*
   Criers and Kibitzers, Kibitzers and Criers.

   The Dick Gibson Show.
   The MacGuffin.
   The Magic Kingdom.
ANNIE ERNAUX, *Cleaned Out.*
LAUREN FAIRBANKS, *Muzzle Thyself.*
   Sister Carrie.
LESLIE A. FIEDLER,
   Love and Death in the American Novel.
RONALD FIRBANK, *Complete Short Stories.*
FORD MADOX FORD, *The March of Literature.*
JANICE GALLOWAY, *Foreign Parts.*
   The Trick Is to Keep Breathing.
WILLIAM H. GASS, *The Tunnel.*
   Willie Masters' Lonesome Wife.
ETIENNE GILSON, *The Arts of the Beautiful.*
C. S. GISCOMBE, *Giscome Road.*
   Here.
KAREN ELIZABETH GORDON, *The Red Shoes.*
PATRICK GRAINVILLE, *The Cave of Heaven.*
GEOFFREY GREEN, ET AL., *The Vineland Papers.*
HENRY GREEN, *Concluding.*
   Nothing.
JIŘÍ GRUŠA, *The Questionnaire.*
JOHN HAWKES, *Whistlejacket.*
ALDOUS HUXLEY, *Antic Hay.*
   Point Counter Point.
   Those Barren Leaves.
   Time Must Have a Stop.
GERT JONKE, *Geometric Regional Novel.*
TADEUSZ KONWICKI, *A Minor Apocalypse.*
   The Polish Complex.
ELAINE KRAF, *The Princess of 72nd Street.*
EWA KURYLUK, *Century 21.*
DEBORAH LEVY, *Billy and Girl.*
JOSÉ LEZAMA LIMA, *Paradiso.*
OSMAN LINS, *The Queen of the Prisons of Greece.*
ALF MAC LOCHLAINN,
   The Corpus in the Library.
   Out of Focus.
D. KEITH MANO, *Take Five.*
BEN MARCUS, *The Age of Wire and String.*
WALLACE MARKFIELD, *Teitlebaum's Window.*
   To an Early Grave.
DAVID MARKSON, *Collected Poems.*
   Reader's Block.
   Springer's Progress.
   Wittgenstein's Mistress.
CARL R. MARTIN, *Genii Over Salzburg.*
CAROLE MASO, *AVA.*
HARRY MATHEWS, *Cigarettes.*
   The Conversions.

Visit our website: www.dalkeyarchive.com

DALKEY ARCHIVE PAPERBACKS

Visit our website: www.dalkeyarchive.com